Also by Deborah D. Moore

The Journal Series
Cracked Earth
Ash Fall
Crimson Skies
Raging Tide
Fault Line
Martial Law

A Prepper's Cookbook

EMPulse
EMPulse 2

TIME
SHADOWS

DEBORAH D. MOORE

PERMUTED
PRESS

A PERMUTED PRESS BOOK
ISBN: 978-1-68261-486-0
ISBN (eBook): 978-1-68261-487-7

Time Shadows

Cover art by Christian Bentulan

PERMUTED
PRESS

Permuted Press, LLC
New York • Nashville
permutedpress.com

Published in the United States of America

This is for my brother Tom, a magical person in my life.

If your absence doesn't affect them
Your presence never mattered.
—unknown

ACKNOWLEDGEMENTS

------◆------

I have two of the best beta readers: my brother Tom and my son Eric. They give me incredible help with suggestions and clarifications and encouragement. So thank you both.

An extra thank you to my son Eric, for something that eludes me - maintaining my website: deborahdmoore.com, where you can find a full listing of all of my books.

A special shout out to the art department at Permuted Press for all the awesome book covers. And to the staff there that keeps everything moving forward.

PROLOGUE

---•◉•---

Morgan sat quietly on the floor in front of the low altar, watching the snow fall outside the mirror window. Her silky, dark hair falling across her face like a veil. She closed her eyes and passed her hand over the small deep blue crystal resting in the center of the symbols etched on the ancient wooden table. Visions seeped into her mind and she focused, opening her eyes to materialize the images. The tall dark haired girl in front of her was the one. Now, all she had to do was find her, no matter how long it took.

CHAPTER ONE

————◆————

Sage Aster sat alone on the park bench, contemplating her predicament and her life in general. A salty tear rolled down her wind bruised cheek and she quickly wiped it away. Her predicament was easy: it was late September; she was almost broke and now homeless. Her life, however, was a bit more complicated.

At twenty-six and fresh out of college with a Master's degree in History, Sage used up a good portion of her miniscule savings to get an apartment near the Museum of History and Arts where she had been lucky to find work. Although all she did was research the old catalogs and update the information into a computer, it was a job and it was in her field with room for advancement, something very few of her classmates could claim. Then she got the phone call from her sister: their parents had been in a serious accident and she had to come home—now.

It was the weekend and everyone she needed to inform she had a family emergency was out of town and not reachable. Sage closed up her apartment, left word with an acquaintance in the personnel department at the museum, and caught the first bus back to Michigan.

Her parents died before she could say goodbye. Distraught as she was, Sage shouldered the responsibility of closing the meager estate. Meager was a generous term. It seemed that her folks had taken numerous home equity loans to continuously fund her sister's selfish lifestyle. There was only enough equity left in the quaint old house to pay for the burial, and when her sister found out there wasn't anything left, she vanished.

Six weeks after her parents died, Sage was on a bus back to New York expecting to pick up the pieces of her life. What Sage didn't expect, was her co-worker failed to inform management of her emergency, and she was fired as a no-show. On top of that, someone had stripped her apartment of everything she owned, and the leasing company, thinking she had moved out —even though the rent was current—rented it to a new tenant.

With only five-hundred dollars remaining in her pocket from a small life insurance policy, she was at a loss for what to do. Staying at the YWCA was better than shivering on a park bench, but only barely. That would come later; for now, she closed her eyes to the brightness and let the afternoon sun warm her face, her small wheeled suitcase secure between her feet.

"You look like you could use a friend," Morgan said, sitting down on the other end of the old wooden bench.

Sage was startled by the soft voice. Sure it had come from someone old and wise, she was surprised to see a very pretty thirty-something woman sitting three feet away. The young woman had creamy, translucent skin and long black hair with eyes so brown they almost matched her hair. A long, dark skirt skimmed the fashionable boots and added to the mysterious apparition.

"I don't think even a best friend would want to hear my problems," Sage frowned, and closed her eyes again. She reached into her jacket pocket for her lip balm, a nervous habit she picked up from her mother.

"Try me," the woman stated sincerely. "By the way, my name is Morgan; Morgan Alsteen." She held out her hand to the younger girl.

Sage looked at the extended hand and felt a strange compulsion to take it. Laying her small hand against the exposed flesh of the

2

friendly person beside her, she felt a tingle up to her elbow. "I'm Sage Aster." And she began to talk.

———————◆———————

"Oh, my, you have been through quite the ordeal lately," Morgan said when Sage finally stopped to take a breath. She stood, producing an old gnarled cane and leaned heavily on it. "With the sun going down it's getting too cold to sit here. I promised someone a long time ago, that I would repay a kindness done to me when I needed it, so I'm going to offer you a safe roof over your head and a hot meal. However long you decide to stay will be up to you."

"Are you serious?" Sage said, getting to her feet to face her new benefactor.

"Oh, I'm quite serious, Sage. I always repay my debts. Come, let's go home." Morgan, being almost as tall as Sage, easily slid her arm into the crook of the girl's and led her to the curb, where she lifted her cane and instantly a taxi cab swerved to pick them up. She gave the cab driver an address on the Upper West Side, and he pulled back into the heavy afternoon traffic.

———————◆———————

When the cab pulled into a cobblestone driveway and faced closed gates, Morgan produced a small device, and the gates opened.

"If you would pull under the portico, I would appreciate it," she said. As the driver jumped out of the cab and opened her door, she handed him a one-hundred-dollar bill and whispered inaudibly. He acquired a puzzled, blank look, stuck the bill in a pocket and drove away.

"Aren't you afraid he's going to remember you being so generous and come back to rob you?" Sage asked.

Morgan chuckled, knowing the cab driver already had lost his memory of the trip, the address, and the rich lady. "Is that your only bag?" she asked, fending off the question.

"Yeah, I learned real fast that I had to keep everything with me unless I wanted to lose it. The YWCA isn't known for its security," Sage scoffed. "Fortunately, all I lost there was most of my clothes."

"If I may ask, what is in your case that is valuable to you?"

"A few pictures of my parents, some memento's, their wedding rings...and legal papers: their death certificates, my diploma, stuff like that." Sage looked around the foyer they had entered. "Wow. This place is huge—a real mansion! Are you sure you want a stranger staying here?" The foyer, with a polished slate floor and golden honey wood paneling, was bigger than her kitchen—former kitchen.

"Ah, I don't see you as a stranger, though, Sage. You're my new best friend. Let me show you your room. Henry!" she called out and an older man appeared as if out of thin air. "Henry, this is Miss Sage Aster, she will be staying here for a while. Please take her bag to the..." Morgan looked back at Sage, "...peach room."

"Peach is my favorite color!"

"I know," Morgan murmured. "Henry, once you're done, will you please tell Alyce the two of us will have dinner in the library in a half hour." They slowly climbed the long graceful staircase with Henry at the lead.

———————— ✦ ————————

Sage carefully watched where she was being led so she could escape quickly if she had to. Chances like this often came with strings attached. She placed her few items of clothing in the dresser, leaving her most precious belongings in her small suitcase in the event she had to leave on a moment's notice. In time, she would be amused with those early thoughts, although for now, she felt the need to be cautious.

She washed her hands and face with the sweet-smelling herbal soap in the luxurious bathroom connected to her pale-peach bed-room. "Suite" was a better term for the room, that also had a sitting room with a fireplace and an outside covered and screened porch that further connected the two rooms. She hung the towel up and gazed longingly at the oversized bathtub, determined to make use of it later.

"I see you've found your way back here. Good! The many hall-ways in this big old house can be confusing," Morgan greeted her.

"Big is an understatement."

"Yes, and with ten bedrooms, five of them suites, and all of them with private baths, it does qualify as a mansion," Morgan shrugged. "That's ten on the second level. The servants have their own suites in the other wing."

"Is this the library?" Sage questioned, looking around, trying to not be overwhelmed.

"No, merely a greeting room," Morgan smiled. "The library is down the hall. First though, I'd like an aperitif. Would you join me in a touch of Campari? And would you pour, please. My hands aren't as steady as they once were. How do you like your room, Sage?"

"It's beautiful, thank you. I think my entire apartment could easily fit into those two rooms!" Sage poured the clear red liquid from the heavy crystal decanter.

"It's nice to have someone here to appreciate the place," Morgan said. "Tomorrow, perhaps, we'll take a walk around the yards. Henry does a good job of making sure the grounds are well-tended." She sipped from the small crystal glass, watching Sage from over the rim.

"Dinner awaits you, ma'am," Henry announced and then dis-appeared again.

"Good. I don't know about you, but I'm hungry," Morgan said, once again holding onto Sage's arm as she guided them down the wide hallway, their footfalls silenced by the thick dark carpeting.

CHAPTER TWO

———————⁕———————

"**N**ice," Sage commented, admiring the vaulted ceiling and the worn leather bindings on the nearest book shelf.

"This is my favorite room. I dine here often. The formal dining room is much too large and ostentatious for one person. If I'm not engrossed in reading, I usually eat in the kitchen, even though it makes Alyce nervous," Morgan chuckled.

"So how many of these books have you actually read?" Sage asked with a snicker.

"Every single one," Morgan answered simply. "I hope you like chicken."

They settled into two sturdy wooden chairs facing each other across the small cloth-draped table. A rolling cart with covered platters sat beside them, a bottle of Chardonnay cooled in a leather bucket of ice.

"I hope you don't mind me imposing on you to serve both of us. As I said, my hands aren't as steady as they once were."

"Hey, it's the least I can do," she lifted a silver dome to find a pecan coated chicken breast nestled in a bed of rice pilaf, three stalks of asparagus with thin strips of roasted red sweet pepper, and three cucumber medallions with sauce drizzled on top. Wide eyed, she set the platter in front of Morgan and took the second one for herself.

Without being asked, Sage then poured them each a glass of wine, and sat back down to eat.

Morgan took a bite of the chicken and silently watched Sage devour her meal.

"That was one of the best meals I've ever had," Sage touched the white linen napkin to her lips when she was finished.

"I'm pleased you enjoyed the food. I give Alyce free rein in the kitchen and she loves to experiment. Sometimes the chicken is coated with crushed walnuts or almonds instead of pecans, whatever she feels like using. The only thing I insist on is the vegetables must be fresh from one of our greenhouses." She stood and walked over to the small side bar. "Let's have a glass of sherry and enjoy the fire while we talk." A slight wave of her hand ignited the wood stacked inside the large fire pit behind Sage.

Sage turned at the sound of the crackling blaze, wondering how she could have missed the fire burning so brightly. She accepted the small glass of ruby liquid, and sat in one of the two over-stuffed armchairs facing the fire, thinking she may have stepped through the looking glass.

"Tell me about your apartment. What did you lose? Did the management company at least return your deposit?" Morgan quizzed her gently.

"I lost everything. Most of the furniture was used and cheap. The biggest loss was my books…and my clothes. I guess I should go shopping in the next few days," she swirled the wine and took a sip. "And the management company said the deposit barely covered the damage to the door. I'll need to find a job soon. That's my greatest loss; I had a nice position at the Museum of History and Art. With a Master's degree in history, it was the perfect job."

"So, you're a history buff?" Morgan mulled that over when Sage nodded. "History is my passion also. It might be a bit premature, Sage, but I'd like to offer you a job, here, as my companion; kind of like a personal assistant. I'm finding it more and more difficult to get around on my own, and I don't like going out by myself. There is so much to see in this city: the theater, Broadway, the museums, and it's just not fun going alone." When Sage didn't respond, she continued. "How about we give it a trial of say two weeks, and you can decide after that."

"I...I guess that would be okay. Thank you, Morgan."

"Do you think you can find your way back to your room on your own? My quarters are by necessity on the main floor." Morgan simply walked out the library door without waiting for an answer.

Sage took the remaining half bottle of Chardonnay and a wine glass and headed upstairs to that big bathtub.

CHAPTER THREE

———————————◆————————————

"**G**ood morning, Sage. I hope you slept well," Morgan said when Sage wandered into what had been referred to as a greeting room. It was a large room, with multiple seating arrangements, including a table near the floor-to-ceiling windows. On closer inspection, Sage noticed the windows were actually doors that led to a closed off sun room.

"Better than I expected." The tantalizing aromas wafting in her direction caused her mouth to water and she turned toward the side tables where a breakfast buffet was laid out. "Can I refresh your coffee, Morgan?" She was quickly becoming accustomed to serving Morgan. Assessing that feeling, she found it didn't *feel* like serving, more like assisting, helping, her.

"Thank you, I'd appreciate that." Morgan had planted a seed of helpfulness over dinner the night before, and was pleased that it had taken root so quickly, and that her power was still strong.

Sage helped herself to a little bit of eggs, bacon, sausage, and then added a buttered biscuit. She took her place across from her new friend and ate in silence.

"I know I promised a tour of the gardens today, that may have to wait until after lunch, though," Morgan explained. "This morning my personal shopper is stopping by to meet you and assess what clothing you need."

Sage looked up from her plate, the full fork poised mid-way. "I can't afford…"

"This isn't something you need to afford, it's your first two weeks of wages as my personal assistant, and trust me, I *can* afford it," Morgan interrupted to assure her. "If you are going to be out with me, even if it's for only two weeks, you need to be properly dressed. We certainly can't have you wearing jeans and a sweatshirt to a Broadway show!"

Sage nodded and, embarrassed, said nothing further.

———— ·❋· ————

"Mister Lyle has arrived, ma'am," Henry announced.

Morgan looked to Sage, "You're going to like Lyle Jones. He has remarkable fashion sense and a delightful sense of humor!"

Half an hour after Morgan left them alone, she could hear the two laughing, and decided to check Lyle's progress.

"Ah, Morgan!" Lyle said smiling. "This young lady is going to be a breeze to outfit. She's a perfect size eight, with her dark hair and blue eyes she has autumn coloring, and, most importantly, I *like* her!" He picked up his swatch book and announced, "I'll be back in a few hours with the first selection," and he left to shop.

"Well, that was quite the experience," Sage said once he was gone.

"I knew you'd like him. Let me show you the rest of the house and then the greenhouses. The grounds aren't really much to look at this time of year however I'm sure you'll enjoy the rest."

They wandered through the big house while Morgan explained the history. "The house was built in the early 1900's by a wealthy doctor. He had high hopes of a large family, however he died in the Spanish Flu epidemic before his young wife had any children. She left the place to someone she befriended; they in turn befriended me, and now I have it." Morgan stretched the truth hoping it would suffice.

"It certainly is big," Sage commented.

"You are welcome to explore on your own. Only my private quarters are off limits, even to the staff," Morgan said, setting the necessary boundaries.

The days passed quickly. Lyle filled Sage's walk in closet with a variety of clothes, coats, and shoes. Then she finally had an opportunity to use some.

"Did you enjoy the show, Sage?" Morgan asked after the waiter had poured the four of them some wine, and left with their order.

"Enjoy it? It was magnificent! I had read about *Cats* for years, but never thought I would ever get to see it on Broadway!" her eyes lit with excitement. "I was totally fascinated with the Siamese cat! Did you see her? She has to have cats at home; she was so...so cat-like! The way she sat in the background and *groomed*, and then curled up on a step, and..."

"But she didn't have any speaking, or singing, parts," Lyle interrupted.

"I agree with Sage: she was very cat like, and our cat doesn't talk at all," Jon Tippon grinned, and winked at his partner. "I think we were very fortunate to even get tickets. I hear the show is sold out for the next eighteen months."

"It pays to plan ahead," Morgan said, knowing she had used her magical powers to make the four tickets available for purchase, the same as she had gotten them a table at a very busy restaurant to top off their evening. She needed to win Sage's trust and loyalty, and soon.

The cab dropped Lyle and Jon off at their apartment, and continued on to the upper West Side. As before, the driver was tipped well, and quickly forgot his generous ride.

"I hope you don't mind if I don't join you for a nightcap, Sage. I'm feeling exceptionally tired tonight."

"Sleep well, Morgan, and thank you for an incredible evening," Sage responded before climbing the stairs to her own rooms.

* * * ❂ * * *

The days and weeks passed in a similar fashion. Dining out at exclusive restaurants was a frequent activity, as was wandering the museums and seeing off Broadway productions. Sage grew comfortable in her new life. Feeling fortunate she had met Morgan was an understatement.

CHAPTER FOUR

———◆———

"What's this?" Sage asked, looking at the envelope beside her breakfast plate.

"That must be your apartment security deposit," Morgan said. "I hope it's all right that I had someone look into that leasing company. My sources got to the core quickly. There wasn't any damage to your door, Sage; the lock had been picked. The leasing company realized it was in their best interest to promptly refund your deposit and unused rent. At least now, you have some pocket money."

Sage opened the envelope and saw the check from the apartment holding company: her full three months' refund. "Thank you. It hadn't occurred to me to question them. Excuse me." Overwhelmed with Morgan's generous nature, she left the table without eating and headed to her new favorite place: the greenhouse that was more like a solarium, and was filled with a variety of colorful flowers in different stages of blossoming. An artificial waterfall surrounded with wooden benches was the centerpiece of the large glass dome where she sat. She smoothed the soft fine brown wool of her new slacks and crossed her ankles. A tear slipped down and splashed on the warm, forest-green turtleneck cashmere sweater.

"Is everything all right, Sage?" Morgan asked softly. "I was hoping you would be pleased with your windfall."

Sage looked up, ignoring the tears on her cheeks. "I *am* pleased, Morgan, truly I am. It's that this, all of this, everything you've done for me, is so overwhelming, and I don't know how to begin to thank you."

Now is the time, Morgan thought. "I can think of a way. There is something I need done that I can't do, and don't worry, it's not illegal. I would never allow any harm to come to you."

"Anything."

"Be careful how quickly you agree," Morgan chuckled. "Tell me, Sage, how old do you think I am?"

"I'm terrible at guessing. You look in your early thirties, although you seem older, sometimes much older."

"Could you accept that I'm almost eight hundred years old?"

Sage laughed at the absurdity. "No, there is no way anyone is that old."

"Do you believe in magic?" Morgan continued, ignoring her comment.

"I don't know. I can't recall ever having anything I would consider being magical happen to me."

"Not even tickets to a sold-out show, or a new friend arriving right when you need one?"

"Are you trying to tell me you're a witch or something?" Sage scoffed.

"No, I'm not a witch; witches are not immortal and they use potions and spells. I'm a sorceress. And I'm very powerful, if I do say so myself. And I *am* very old. I was born on December 21, 1221. Adding that the date is also the winter solstice, 12-21-1221 is a very strong combination. While I may use spells, my power comes from within *me*," she explained. "You don't believe me, do you?"

"Let's say I'm skeptical," Sage smiled even though she was feeling deep sorrow. Morgan must be very ill to have such delusions, and that saddened her deeply.

"Of course, you are. I would be disappointed in you if you immediately accepted my tale. Nonetheless, Sage, it *is* true."

"And what is it that you need me to do for you that you can't do yourself? As a powerful sorceress, can't you do everything?"

"Not everything." Morgan stood and lifted her cane; the hard benches suddenly had soft pillows, done in a pale green and beige plaid. "That's better, my butt was getting sore." And she sat again. "Now, let me explain pieces of my life and how you can help me."

"Can I get you anything first? Water? Tea?" Sage offered, thinking she must have missed the pillows earlier.

Morgan waved her hand and a cart appeared. "Tea would be nice. You can pour."

The cart materializing startled Sage, though she figured it was a trick, and taking that in stride, she nonchalantly poured two cups of tea.

"As a young sorceress, I grew greedy for power, and I did anything and everything to get it. What is that saying Baron Acton wrote back in 1887? 'Power corrupts, and absolute power corrupts absolutely.' That was me. I did some very bad things, some very mean things, and why? *Because I could.*"

"I don't believe that. You're not a mean person, Morgan," Sage said.

"But I *was*, Sage! And now I want to make amends. I want to set some things right. Will you help me?"

"And how could I do that?"

"I can send you back in time to right those wrongs," Morgan said with conviction.

"Back in time? As in time travel? Why don't *you* go back?"

"I can't be *when* I already am."

"I don't understand."

"I can't cross paths with myself, one of us will cease to exist, and because I am more powerful now than I was before, my other self would end and if that happens, then my *now* self will also cease to exist."

"Oh, that certainly wouldn't be good."

"However, I can send *you* back to stop me from doing certain key things."

"Wouldn't I cease to exist too?"

"No, you would be going back to a time before you were born." Morgan shifted on the pillows. "See, that's my paradox, I've been alive for eight hundred years and there's no timeline that will help where I don't already exist. Will you do this for me?"

"Yeah, why not?" Sage thought that if humoring Morgan would help her pay her debt, then so be it. "What do I do?"

CHAPTER FIVE

———⊛———

Morgan waved her gnarly old cane at the door to her quarters and the door swung open, exposing a large sitting room. Sage had watched enough science fiction movies to know that there could be, and likely was, hidden sensors that had been activated to open the door. She followed Morgan into the forbidden rooms.

The ancient sorceress looked at Sage, taking in her clothes and footwear. Good, not much adjustment would be needed, perhaps only an additional jacket. The suede boots were classic and would not be noticed in any timeline. Lyle would be commended, and compensated, later for his selection. "There is a jacket on the back of that chair, you may need it."

Sage picked up the heavy brown and green tweed jacket she hadn't noticed earlier and slipped it on; it was a perfect fit and went remarkably well with what she was already wearing. They passed a small bed, filled with fluffy pillows and stood in front of a blank wall.

"Now, we are going into my most private of rooms. Please, my dear, keep an open mind, it will make things easier," Morgan again lifted her cane, then lowered it and turned back to face Sage. "Conjuring concealment is one of the most basic of all spells." She waved the staff at the wall and a door appeared; she flipped her hand and the door opened, exposing a large room, and stepped in, beckoning Sage to follow.

Wide-eyed and hesitant, Sage entered and the door disappeared behind them.

The room was massive with a vaulted ceiling and ancient looking yet colorful wall tapestries that depicted various scenes that seemed to move. The room itself was sixty-foot square with a deeply polished oak floor, and no furniture, save for the low desk in front of a large gold-leafed mirror.

"Sage, I'm not going to hurt you, I promise! The thing about you that is going to be our greatest asset is your knowledge of history. It will allow you to blend in and 'go with the flow' wherever you land."

"Wherever I land? You don't know where I'm going?" Sage decided to play along with Morgan's delusion.

"Approximately; However, you will need to make a number of trips to make things right. This first trip will be fairly recent and will last only a few minutes. Take in your surroundings, mentally record your observations; it will help me refine the incantation to be more precise next time.

"Before we start, you need further background information. What I said earlier is true: my power is within me; however, the Star Stone, this blue crystal, is a conduit, an amplifier if you will. There are only three in existence. One is fused with my staff—think of it as a Harry Potter wand on steroids. The other two are less conspicuous and are worn as jewelry." She touched the base of her wrist and stroked the head of the golden, enchanted serpent; it yawned and let go of its tail, coiling into Morgan's hand. The small, dime-sized deep blue crystal stone dangled around its neck. "I want you to wear this: it will bring you home when you've completed your task. No one can remove it, not even you, so don't worry about losing it." She took the living creature, looped its body around Sage's neck, and when she fed the serpent its own tail, it once again stilled and turned to solid gold. "The only warning you will get that you are about to shift and return home, is the stone will get very warm against your skin."

"Where did the stones come from?" Sage asked, fingering the cool stone, sure what looked like a living snake was an illusion.

"From the stars," Morgan said smiling.

"Okay, where did *you* get them?"

"From my mentor. The staff was hers, as well as the other two stones. She trained two of us: myself and…Evon. She was very old, a thousand years at least, was ready to die, and wanted to pass on the wisdom of the Art."

"Where is Evon?"

"That's for another time, Sage. Are you ready? Stand here," she pointed to a spot on the floor. With her staff held a foot off the floor, she drew a circle of flame around Sage who recoiled. "Don't be afraid, this is not a flame of fire; it's a flame of faith—*my* faith." She chanted a few words and drew another, larger circle, then intersecting lines and more circles within. Morgan moved around the outer lines, seeming to float. Sage heard words being spoken that she couldn't understand.

"How will I know what this task is and what to do?" Sage called out.

Morgan stopped across from Sage, twenty feet away. "There is something you need to fix where you're going. Believe in the impossible and let it guide you." She crossed her hands in front of herself and then flung her hands out to the sides, as a final gesture. Sage disappeared.

Sage bumped into a low wooden chaise lounge and gazed out at the ocean, the brisk breeze ruffled her short dark hair. She looked around to see she was on a large ship of some sort. Her stomach suddenly convulsed and she bent over a potted plant and vomited up tea and bile. She spit once again, trying to regain her balance and clear her woozy head.

"You did it Morgan, you really did it!" As she straightened up, she spotted the life ring hanging on the bulkhead beside her and she went still. "Oh, great! I'm on the fucking *Titanic*!" and she sat hard on the low chair.

CHAPTER SIX

---- ✳ ----

"**P**lease, sir, watch your language!"

Sage spun around to see a young woman, with blonde hair swept high on her head, sitting on an identical chaise lounge a few feet away, an open book in her lap. Her feet and legs were covered with a heavy black and red plaid blanket. "My apologies," Sage said.

"I did not see you arrive. I guess I was too deeply engrossed in my reading," she replied, eying Sage. "Wait, you're not a boy. You are a girl...why are you dressed like a man, and what happened to your hair?" she blurted out.

Sage looked back at the ocean, the ship and a few people strolling. It was April, 1912, one hundred and eight years in her past, and she was on the doomed *Titanic*. "Ah, I've been a bit under the weather, and I find trousers are much warmer than skirts." She was careful not to call them pants.

"And what about your hair? It's so...short!"

"That's rather embarrassing," Sage smiled shyly while trying to think of something. Noticing the book in the young woman's lap, she remembered a story she read a few years back with a similar situation. "I was visiting my friend, Camille, in the south of France. Her younger sister, Sarah, was offended that I wished to speak with Camille without the child around. That night Sarah put thistle burrs

22

in my hair while I slept. By morning everything was so tangled it was impossible to comb it out."

"My goodness! What did you do?"

"Camille's mother hired a barber from the city to come to the villa…and the only solution he had was to cut my hair off to get rid of the burrs and style it short like a man's. That was two months ago, so it's actually longer than I started with." Sage finished her impossible tale, hoping it was believable. "I left shortly after that when that evil child wasn't even punished for her behavior."

"You poor dear! I'm Lady Helen Christina Woodhaven," she held out her hand. "And you are…?"

"I'm Sage Aster. Pleased to make your acquaintance, Lady Woodhaven," Sage shook her hand, as she would anyone else. Her firm handshake seemed to startle the other woman for some reason.

"Miss Astor, it is I who am pleased to meet *you*," Helen said, mistaking her for one of the famous and wealthy Astor's aboard.

The historian in Sage quickly understood what had just happened, and she felt it best to not correct the error. She was still trying to come to grips with the fact that Morgan had indeed sent her to the past and that everything she said about being a sorceress was true!

"So, what are you reading, Lady Woodhaven?" Sage asked in an attempt to shift the conversation away from her.

"Oh, I recently found a new author, and I predict he's going to become quite famous: Norman Bean! Have you heard of him? His book, *Under the Moon of Mars*, came out several weeks ago. I was lucky to get a copy before we departed Southampton."

"Norman Bean?" Sage mulled the name over. "Oh, that's Edgar Rice Burroughs; Bean is his pen name."

"I didn't know this," Helen seemed momentarily subdued while she absorbed this new piece of information.

"You are correct though, he's destined for greatness," Sage assured her. "Whom else do you enjoy reading?"

"Well, there is Jules Verne and Herbert Wells, both with fascinating imaginations. Have you read either of them?" When Sage nodded, she continued, "Wonderful! I now have someone to talk to about them. My brother, Ethan, thinks I'm filling my head with silly nonsense. So does my husband," she looked down and frowned. "If he, my husband that is, insists I refrain from this fictional reading, then I suppose I will have to do as he bids." She frowned again. "I am hoping for an understanding husband though."

Sage chuckled, "You don't know yet if he is understanding or not?"

"Oh, no, you see, I haven't met him yet. My father, Lord Woodhaven, made all the arrangements and sent me, and my dowry, on this trip to America with my brother to watch over both," she mumbled. "But I digress. Until we arrive in New York, I am still free to read whatever I wish. Do you read much, Miss Astor?"

"Yes, I read quite a bit, Lady Woodhaven."

"Please, call me Helen."

"Only if you call me Sage."

"I'm honored...Sage," and Helen smiled brightly, showing perfect white teeth.

"Excuse me, Lady Woodhaven, is this bloke bothering you?" the steward asked, scowling at Sage.

"Oh, Arnold, this is *Miss* Sage Astor, my new best friend. Would you please get her a lap blanket and then bring us both a pot of tea and some biscuits?" Helen ordered the attendant.

"Certainly, ma'am, and my apologies Miss Astor, please forgive me," he blinked rapidly, bowed and departed.

Well, that was an interesting exchange, Sage thought. This is without any doubt, First Class.

"So tell me, Helen, what did you think of the Jules Verne classic, *Twenty Thousand Leagues under the Sea*?"

"I'm not sure it will be a classic, but it was certainly fanciful!

Ships that run under the water we've already seen with the Germans and their U-boats, however men walking on the ocean floor is quite hard to believe," Helen replied.

"I see it happening; why not? If we can imagine it, it can come to be. We will have to discuss that one a bit further, another time though. What else have you read?" Sage pushed the subject, trying to figure out this frightfully young woman who was on her way to meet the man she was to marry. "You seem to prefer scientific fiction. What about the H.G. Wells book, *The Time Machine?*"

Helen clapped her hands in glee. "What an amazing story. The thought of being able to travel to another time is intriguing, don't you think?"

"You have no idea," Sage muttered. "What would you do, if you could travel back in time?"

The steward returned at that moment with a covered tray and set it on a small table between the two women. He removed a blanket from over his arm and hesitantly draped it across Sage's legs and backed away, watching her curiously. "Will there be anything else?" he asked.

"Thank you, no," Helen piped in, dismissing the man and removed the cloth covering the tray to expose a china teapot, two delicate cups, and a plate of frosted cookies. The steward gratefully departed.

Sage realized how hungry she was when she got a whiff of the sweet frosting. It took a great deal of restraint not to grab a couple and devour them. Next time, she vowed to finish her breakfast.

"Let's see," Helen tipped her head thinking. "To answer your question, I believe I would go back to a few months ago and protest my marriage to Humphrey Tuttle II. I think I could have talked my father out of it; however, I didn't even try."

"You're not married yet, perhaps you can still get out of it," Sage suggested, wondering if this is what she was sent here to…fix.

"I *am* married to him. We had surrogate ceremony," Helen frowned.

"I see. What would happen if once you meet each other, you don't like him?"

"I would have no choice but to honor the contract."

"What if *he* doesn't like *you*?"

"Oh, he has the choice of terminating the contract for whatever reason he wishes, before consummation that is. I do not. I doubt he will though, Humphrey was much too interested in my dowry," Helen looked at the pot of tea.

"Your dowry? I presume it's substantial?"

"All of my mother's jewels. I should say all that my father didn't sell after she passed away. My mother was the wealthy one in the family, and she loved to sparkle." Helen looked embarrassed. "Goodness, why am I telling this to you? You must think low of me now."

"Not at all, Helen, and I think you told me because you know, deep inside, you can trust me," Sage covered the younger woman's hand with her own in support.

They chatted idly about books and stories while Sage quelled the rumble in her stomach with cookies and warmed herself with the hot tea.

"I so enjoyed Jules Verne's book, *Journey to the Center of the Earth*. What a lark that one was!" Helen laughed, recalling a few of the more memorable scenes in the book.

"What else do you read?" Sage asked after eating her fourth cookie.

Helen looked around to make sure no one was near to over hear them. "The newspaper!" she whispered. "I find the stock market page particularly fascinating." She grinned like a child. "I have even pretended to invest and what I've selected has done quite well. Of course, I can't really invest; it isn't appropriate for a woman of my status to do such things."

"You could have your brother invest for you," Sage suggested.

"Yes, and he would do that for me. However, I don't have any money of my own—only my dowry and that becomes Humphrey's." Helen's matter of fact attitude surprised Sage. "Well, it's getting quite chilly out here. I should return to my rooms."

Sage then had an idea to solve a problem that was quickly surfacing. "Before you go, could you leave me your lap blanket? It's going to get very cold out here tonight."

"You don't intend to *sleep* out here, do you?" Helen was aghast.

"I had quite the argument with my...Uncle John. He dislikes my wearing these warmer trousers, and he also dislikes my reading habits. He has locked me out of our cabins and vowed to ignore me at meals until I capitulate! So, I'm not sure what I'm going to do, except sleep out here tonight."

"You will do no such thing, Sage. I have an idea," Helen said. "Why don't you stay with me for a few days while Colonel Astor calms down? I have a rather large suite, and I believe some of my dresses will fit you, though they may be a bit short, and you will dine with me and Ethan." She stood as though the matter was settled.

"That is rather generous of you Helen. Perhaps if Uncle JJ sees me in a dress it will soften him some," Sage smiled. At least, she won't be sleeping out in the cold on a deck chair tonight.

"Uncle JJ?"

Sage snickered. "He's actually a second cousin, and he hates when I call him that, so I do it to annoy him."

Helen seemed delighted with the piece of private news about one of the more notable passengers. "Men can be such complicated creatures and yet so simple."

CHAPTER SEVEN

———————•❋•———————

"**T**hese are quite nice rooms, Helen," Sage said, looking around the spacious cabin. "I was a last-minute guest of my uncle JJ's young wife and was relegated to the au pair's room. It's small but warm and private."

"This suite adjoins Ethan's rooms through that door," Helen pointed. "I keep this side locked, requiring him to knock before entering. He may be older than I and my brother, but he's still a man."

"That is quite wise. While men seem to enjoy keeping us women in our place, now and then, it's good to remind them they have a place also!" Sage said. All of her reading on the past was helping her with the vernacular of the age, though keeping it up was difficult and getting tiresome.

"Oh, I do like how you think!" Helen giggled. "Now, let's find a suitable dress for you to wear to dinner." She opened the door to what was a small bedroom, presumably for a child or a maid. Dresses hung from available hooks and were also laid out on the small bed. "We will have to straighten this room for you to sleep here. For now though, let us find you something other than trousers."

Sage looked at the long frilly dresses and winced. *It's only for dinner—a few hours at the most*, she reminded herself.

"Do you have a favorite color?" Helen continued.

"Peach, dark tan, green, and blue is good too," she replied, thinking of her peach bedroom in Morgan's house, silently wondering if Morgan knew where—and when—she was.

Helen picked up and discarded several dresses, then handed Sage a silk dress in deep teal-blue. "This one matches your eyes. However, this green one would look stunning with your dark hair. Try it on."

Sage removed her jacket and draped it on the back of a narrow chair. After removing her heavy sweater, suede boots, and the dark brown pants, she stood in her underwear and socks to pick up the dress.

"Those are very strange undergarments you have, Sage," Helen stared at the lacey bra and equally lacey panties. "Is that a new fashion?"

"Um yes, straight from Paris. A bit risqué for my taste, but they are immensely comfortable," she said, hoping to cover the odd items she had on that to her weren't strange at all. "This dress is lovely!" she slid it over her head and felt the softness caress her skin. The dress had simple, flowing lines of which she approved and no frilly lace. After slipping her arms into the loose sleeves, she noticed the front had strings right below the deep scoop of the neckline, to tighten and make it form fitting. *What women went through just to get dressed,* she thought.

"A waist petticoat should be all you need. Even though the fashion is now for slimmer skirts, I still prefer full ones, and this one fits you well. Even the length is acceptable: not too much of your shoes will be showing," Helen walked around Sage. "What a most intriguing necklace that is! It seems to have changed color to match the dress. What is it?"

"It's called a star stone," Sage gently fingered the stone, and was shocked when she felt the serpent vibrate around her neck as though it was purring. "What dress are you going to wear for dinner?" she asked, putting her comfortable soft boots back on.

"I'm feeling daring, so I think I shall wear the red dress." She picked it up and shook the wrinkles out. "With you wearing such a beautiful necklace, I think I will wear something from my dowry." She took a good sized wooden box from the top drawer of the dresser and opened it, revealing trays of gems.

"Wow…I mean, my goodness, those are stunning. All those were your mother's? Do you get to wear them often?"

"I'm trying to wear as many as I can on this voyage, since it's doubtful I will get to keep them once we arrive. I believe these rubies will go well with my dress." Helen handed Sage the gold necklace inlaid with the large red stones and smaller diamonds. Sage placed it around Helen's neck, as the girl lifted her long blonde hair out of the way. The tiers of gems formed a more than adequate coverage for the young woman's cleavage.

The cool stone resting in the hollow of Sage's neck tingled and grew warm. *What I'm to do must involve her dowry.*

There came a knock on the outer door.

"Come, Helen, we don't want to be late for dinner!" a deep masculine voice announced.

"Ethan can be so impatient!" Helen opened the door to reveal a handsome young blond man that bore a distinct resemblance to her. "Ethan, this is my friend, Sage Astor. Sage, this is my older brother, Lord Ethan Edward Woodhaven."

"It appears that I have two beautiful women to escort to dinner," he said, smiling and locking eyes with Sage. His attention was quickly drawn to the star stone, and a look of recognition passed quickly through his eyes and was then gone. He held out both arms for the women to hold while they walked down the long passageway that led them to the grand staircase and on to the aft dining hall.

Walking carefully down the broad Grand Stairway into the first-class dining hall, the women held their skirts high enough to not trip. Sage quietly gasped at the opulence before her. Several enormous crystal chandeliers were glowing with old-styled electric lights, sending out brilliant prisms to illuminate the room; tables were set with pristine white linens, fine china, and polished silver; crystal goblets of various sizes and use graced each setting. She set her face with the most nonchalant look she could muster and tried to act as though this was all commonplace to her when in fact it was staggering to her overloaded senses.

Ethan led them to a table off to the side that had been thus far unoccupied. Upon sitting, there was immediately a waiter present to pour them some wine and to fill the water goblets. Not long after two more couples joined their table.

Even though introductions had been made, Sage was having difficulty remembering all the names, especially in light of the main topic: ship's gossip. Names flew around the table at lightning speed, leaving her nodding and not participating.

"Please forgive my boldness, Miss Astor, I am quite curious why your hair is so short. It's becoming on you and flatters your face, but it isn't the style these days." One woman asked, one that was the most vicious in her gossip of others.

"Ah, it *is* the style in France and Italy, madam," Sage answered. "I think in a few years it will be quite common in the states, too." At that point, she was saved by the arrival of the first course of raw oysters and assorted hors d'oeuvres.

"You don't like the oysters, Sage?" Ethan politely asked when Sage pushed hers to the side.

"Actually, I have an allergy to them and they upset my stomach. Would you like mine?" she smiled sweetly at him, flirting. The table talk came to a halt; it was unheard of for a single female to share her food with a single male, especially one that was not related to her.

"I'd be delighted," he replied with a sly grin, taking up her challenge—one she didn't know she had issued.

Course after course was served with an elegant flourish. Eventually, the meal was complete and the men departed for their cigars and brandy in the smoking room.

Sage stifled a yawn which Helen noticed.

"I am feeling tired after all the fresh air on the deck this afternoon. Would you care to walk with me to my rooms, Miss Astor?" Helen asked.

"I would be most delighted to," she replied with a grateful smile.

Once out of the main dining room, Helen giggled. "I do think I'm the only one who saw you yawn, Sage! I've no doubt you've had a very long and exhausting day!"

"I certainly have, and thank you for rescuing me from further gossip. I'm sorry to say this, but that woman is an absolute bore!" Sage yawned again.

"I think we should get that bed cleared of my dresses so you can get some sleep," Helen said entering her cabin. "And quite truthfully, I really am tired myself."

"Helen," Sage started. "I want to thank you again for letting me stay here. It shouldn't be much longer that I impose upon you."

"Oh, it's no imposition. I rather like having a friend."

"You don't have any other friends? A nice person like you?"

"That's very kind of you, Sage. Remember though, I'm *Lady* Woodhaven, a title granted me when my mother passed away. It's a class of elites in England, and most of the other *Ladys* I've met are either three times my age, or are snobs, or both!" Helen sighed. "Good night, my friend."

Sage woke confused about her surroundings, until she remembered she was in 1912 and on the doomed *Titanic*. She dressed quickly in the simpler day-dress Helen had left for her and tiptoed out to the tiny bathroom attached to the suite. After washing her face and hands and using the facilities, Sage left Helen a note then quietly exited the rooms and found her way on deck so she could think.

Before leaving Helen's room, she memorized the cabin number so she could find her way back. The ship was huge and with so many passageways she feared she'd get lost.

Sage leaned against the railing and breathed the cold salty air, glad she had slipped on her warm jacket over the dress. The wind ruffled her short hair as the big ship sped on its fatal way.

"Beautiful morning, isn't it?" Ethan said in her ear. He had been very quiet in his approach and startled Sage.

"Yes, it is," she smiled warmly at him to hide her unease. "It's my favorite time of the day, so quiet and peaceful," she said, looking into the deep blue of the early morning sky.

"Very beautiful," Ethan repeated, looking at her and not the sky. "Forgive my boldness, but I feel as if I know you, Sage. Though if we had met before, I surely would remember." His expression became very solemn. "Have you ever had the feeling that you were on the edge of remembering something yet it stayed just out of reach like a shadow? And like your *own* shadow, when you turned to look at it, it moved away?" Sage nodded. "That's what I feel when I look at you, Miss Astor. I know you. I don't know from where or when though, but I do know you, and that is perplexing me."

Sage pulled away from the railing and slipping her arm into his began walking along the mostly empty deck.

"Whenever I've had a déjà vu moment, I try to *not* think about it and eventually it comes to me."

"Wise words from someone so young and beautiful," he smiled down at her, his blond hair falling into his deep brown eyes. A quick, habitual shove with his free hand sent the hair back into place only to fall again.

Sage laughed. "I think we're closer in age than you realize, Lord Woodhaven." Her stomach took a timely moment to gurgle.

"Ah, I've kept you from your breakfast," he laughed. "Come, the buffet should be ready."

"There you are," Helen said, descending the stairs on the aft fourth deck where the breakfast buffet was held. She smiled at Sage and raised her eyebrows at her brother. Although they were seven years apart in age, they had always been close, and she had watched him become handsome and turn into a ladies' man over the last few years, hopping from one affair to the next. Until their mother died; then, he became more devoted to *her*. It was good to see him interested in a woman again.

Sage took a bagel, a smear of cream cheese, and capers then put several long slices of crispy bacon on her plate.

"Don't care for the lox?" Helen asked with a smile.

"I think it's an acquired taste, and I haven't acquired it yet," she replied with a grin. "I prefer bacon."

The three sat at an unoccupied table near an outer window. One of the wait staff quickly brought them a carafe of coffee, a pitcher of orange juice, and filled their water glasses. Sage thought again how extravagant the first-class service was and then turned her attention to her breakfast.

"What are you ladies doing with your day?" Ethan asked, delving into his scrambled eggs.

"I thought it would be great fun to play some shuffleboard," Helen replied. "How about you Sage, are you up for a rousing game of shuffleboard?"

"Why not, since it would be difficult to play a game of bowls," Sage laughed. She had spent some time eavesdropping on conversations ever since she arrived. After several references to bowls, her memory kicked in and realized it was a lawn game much like bocce and had been played in Europe and England for a very long time. It was also one of the few sports women were allowed to partake of.

"Once we settle in America, we must get a game together, provided we can find a suitable green," Ethan said to Sage. His liquid brown eyes held her fast. "Where will you be staying?"

"I'm not sure yet. Oh, dear, here comes that gossip from last night. I think I'll get some air before she sits down. Excuse me." Sage exited out one of the many French doors leading to the outer deck. It wasn't that she couldn't hold her own with the intrusive nature of the woman; she thought it was the best way to avoid Ethan's questions.

———————⋆❂⋆———————

Helen caught up with Sage a few minutes later, and they walked casually around the breezy deck allowing their breakfast to settle.

"I saw a schedule posted yesterday that indicates shuffleboard doesn't begin until after the mid-day meal," Helen said. "What would you like to do before then?"

"I do enjoy the walking. However, anything you would care to do would be fine with me," Sage commented. "We could always sit and talk or find a quiet place to read. I haven't found the lending library as of yet, so that could be something to occupy our time." She casually looked around at the historic ship and in looking up she spotted Ethan gazing down at them. She returned his warm and generous smile, thinking how handsome he was.

"Delightful! I know where it is, and it's a most gracious room. Its dark wood paneling and comfortable furniture, reminds me of my father's library back in England. It's not far from the *Café Parisien* where we can have our mid-day meal," Helen responded. "And the lending library has...newspapers!"

———————— ❋ ————————

"Are you going to wear the blue dress tonight, Sage? I think it will look wonderful on you. It matches your eyes," Helen said, "And that lovely necklace you're wearing. It's simple, yet so elegant. The necklace that is, although the dress is also."

"Thank you. The necklace is very special to me and I think the blue dress would look exceptionally nice. What are you wearing tonight?" Sage put the subject back on Helen.

"I think this yellow dress with the green sash and the emerald necklace." She held up the necklace heavy with finely cut green stones mixed with sparkling diamonds next to the dress lying across the brocade padded chair. She slipped the dress on, and Sage tied the sash in the back in a delicate bow, leaving the ends draping down the full skirt, thinking how much styles had changed. The emerald necklace did indeed compliment the dress well. Sage was feeling overwhelmed by Helen's casualness of wearing such expensive jewelry.

"An excellent choice," Sage smiled at her friend while she slipped the teal blue dress over her head and tied the bodice lacings. There was something nagging her in the back of her mind; something about the date. Before she could ask Helen what the date was, Ethan knocked on the door.

"I see you two lovely ladies are ready for dinner," he smiled warmly at both his sister and at Sage, holding her gaze a few extra seconds. And once again, he held out his arms to escort them to dinner.

As with the previous night, the main dining hall was the epitome of elegance and opulence. The volume of chatting seemed to increase with every passing minute. They were escorted to the same table they had occupied before, and the same two couples were already seated. As Ethan finished seating the women, the sommelier arrived and poured wine for everyone.

The first course of raw oysters came next, and Sage once again slid them in Ethan's direction with a discrete smile.

The meal continued with a choice of creamed soup or consommé, followed by a protein dish of which Sage selected the roast duckling with fresh applesauce and creamed carrots. Afterward, they were all served a demitasse of punch romaine, a palate cleanser of champagne, and shaved ice to prepare them for the main course.

Sage leaned over to Helen and whispered, "I'm quite thankful these portions are small, or I'd be too full to continue." There was something about the meal that was familiar to Sage.

Helen looked at her oddly and said nothing. Helen herself was quite accustomed to meals of multiple, and small, courses. The dining stretched out, taking an undeterminable length of time, and a new wine was offered with each course.

The main dish was perfectly roasted squab, chilled asparagus vinaigrette, and foie gras. When the dessert selection was circulated on a rolling cart, Sage took a small dish of French ice cream that was richer and creamier than anything she had ever had. When the fruits, nuts, and cheeses were presented, she took a few slices of apple to freshen her mouth from all the rich food.

The men once again adjourned to the smoking room for cigars, port, and a few hands of poker while the women retired to the elegant horseshoe-shaped reception room for cordials, where an orchestra softly played.

"Excuse me, Miss Astor," Ethan surprised them all by leaving the men and joining the women, "May I have this dance?" He bowed and held out his hand to her.

"Go on," Helen said smiling, "he's quite the accomplished dancer."

Listening to the soft waltz being played, Sage grinned and took his offered hand. She had been ballroom dancing for most of her life and if he was as good as Helen thought, Sage was about to have some fun.

Ethan started simply, however when he realized Sage was his match, his steps became more intricate. Sage smiled softly at him and whispered, "If you can lead, I can follow."

"Well, then let's give them a show." He moved her around the near empty dance floor with complex and ever changing footwork for nearly fifteen minutes, when the orchestra leader finally ended the song.

Ethan delivered her back to his sister, with a bow and a kiss to the hand. "That was pure heaven for me, Sage. Thank you. Promise you will dance with me every evening of this voyage."

"How can I refuse?" Sage smiled back at him, her heart responding to his sincerity.

"This, April 14, will forever rest in my heart." He kissed her hand again and quickly returned to the smoking room, leaving Sage breathless.

Helen quietly clapped her hands. "Oh, Sage, no one has ever been able to keep up with Ethan! You are most talented."

Gloom passed over Sage's face. "This is April 14?"

"Of course, it is. And since the orchestra has ended, I must presume it's now eleven o'clock."

"Come on, Helen, we must get back to your quarters—we have a lot to talk about." Sage took the young woman's hand and pulling her to her feet, led her out of the elegant room.

CHAPTER EIGHT

———◆———

"**W**hat is so urgent, Sage? You're frightening me," Helen looked harshly at her new friend.

"Good, you need to be scared. Sit down; I have something to tell you." Sage looked around the room. "Do you have any brandy? You might need it by the time I'm done." She had lapsed into her modern-day dialogue.

"What is it you mean?" Helen asked, pointing to a crystal carafe.

Sage nodded, sat down across from Helen and took her hands. "Remember when we first met and talked about books? I asked you about *The Time Machine*. There are things I need to tell you, and I don't have much time, so just listen, okay?" Helen nodded. "Helen, I'm from the future. I was born in 1995. Back home it's 2020."

Helen laughed. "That's preposterous!"

"You will believe me shortly. In a half an hour, this ship will hit an iceberg, and in three hours from now, the *Titanic* will sink."

"This ship is unsinkable!" Helen declared, lifting her chin.

"No ship is unsinkable."

Helen paled. "Am I going to die?"

"Not if I can help it," she tried to reassure her. "I have a friend, a good friend, who asked me to help her right some wrongs and for some reason that involves you." There was a knock on the door. Sage opened it as Helen was visibly shaking.

"May I speak with you, Sage?" Ethan said. "Alone."

"Will the passage way do?" She tried being casual, though she certainly didn't feel that way.

They stepped out into the hallway.

"It's about my sister." Ethan said. "She's quite vulnerable right now and I'm certain you've noticed the jewels she wears."

"Before you go any further, Ethan, I would never harm Helen in any way and no, I am not here to steal her jewels, either, if that's what you're thinking," Sage said angrily, thinking he was hinting in that direction.

Ethan suddenly pulled her into an embrace and kissed her harshly. When Sage relaxed and returned his kiss, he softened and kissed her more gently yet deeply.

"I've wanted to do that ever since I laid eyes on you. There is something about you that draws me to you like a moth to a flame. Even though we've never met, I really do feel as if I know you," he said when he came up for air. "Who are you, Sage Astor? Colonel Astor knows nothing of you."

"I can't tell you anything, however I can ask you to meet us on deck, in a half hour, at lifeboat number eight. Now, go, and dress warmly. Please, just trust me!" She caressed his cheek, gave him a quick kiss and left him stunned, closing the door in his face. Her breathing was heavy and she was equally rattled from what had just happened.

"Please finish this fanciful tale of yours, Sage, and then be gone," Helen lifted her chin in defiance.

Sage was exasperated from being interrupted, and flushed from Ethan's kiss. "This isn't a tale, Helen. To me it's history. The *Titanic* is trying to arrive early in port and is traveling at top speed in an ice field and those in control are ignoring the warnings from other ships in the area. It will hit a berg at 11:40 and will sink at 1:20 in the morning, less than three hours from now. We *must* get you ready for the lifeboat."

"And what would you have me do?" Helen asked defiantly.

"Please, just trust me, this time travel didn't come with an instruction manual. I won't suggest anything you can't undo if I'm wrong." She paced the room a bit. "The star stone warmed when you spoke of your dowry."

"Are you..."

"Damn it, no, I don't want your mother's jewels! *You* need them. Jeez, do you both think I'm a thief?" Sage had a moment of clarity on how to accomplish what was going through her mind. "Come on, let's find you a different dress, one with a higher collar, for warmth and for concealment."

Helen changed into a heavier knit dress with a high scoop neckline with only minor protest. For some unknown reason, she actually believed Sage and trusted her.

"That will have to do. No, don't take that necklace off. In fact, you need to put all these jewels on, and hide them beneath your bodice."

"I'm rightfully alarmed now," Helen said as Sage fastened the last clasp around her neck. "What about the rest? The rings, the earrings, and bracelets, they will show."

"Put them in your pockets." Sage looked her up and down. "Do you have any low-heeled shoes? And what about snacks?"

"Snacks?"

"Biscuits," the difference in terminology was frustrating Sage now that time was slipping away. "It will be a while before help arrives, and you might get hungry while on the life boat."

"In the other room are some I didn't eat, because I don't like the frosting color."

While Helen changed her shoes, Sage laid out a cloth napkin and piled it with the frosted cookies, folding the edges over to form a bag. She tucked the napkin into the pocket of the coat Helen had put on.

"Why are you doing this, Sage?"

She thought for a minute. "Because what I need to do is a kind gesture. One was done to me when I needed it most, as was done to her when she needed. Right now, you need this and, in time, you will need to do a kindness to someone."

"How will I know who?"

"You will know when you meet them, and just go with the flow," Sage smiled as she repeated Morgan's words.

"Can you tell me why I need to hide my jewels?"

"When you meet this new husband of yours, tell him all was lost when the ship went down." The stone warmed on Sage's neck.

"Why would I do that?"

"To see what kind of a man he is. If he doesn't care, and still wants you for his wife, you can tell him the truth. If he rejects you and wanted only your dowry, he will release you from your contract. The jewels are worth a small fortune, and you will never want for anything. You will be free to find a husband that truly loves you." Sage wrapped a heavy scarf around Helen's neck to further hide the necklaces.

"That is an interesting approach. What about Ethan?"

"You can have him invest in the stock market for you," Sage smiled. Sage smacked her head. "Of course! That's one more thing to tell you. Now listen carefully and remember this date." Helen was shocked by Sage's unusual behavior. "In October of 1929, there will be a stock market crash. Investors will lose millions of dollars and it will plunge the country into a depression. I can't tell you the exact date, so be safe and get out of the market slowly, starting in the summer. You don't want to be blamed for the crash or draw attention to yourself, so divest a little at a time. Buy tangibles like gold, and silver, and real estate."

"Real estate?"

"Buy land, they aren't making any more of it," Sage laughed. "I think that was Mark Twain who said that, maybe Will Rogers. I don't remember. Oh, and men will walk not only on the ocean floor, Helen, but on the moon, too."

"Aren't you going to dress warmer?" Helen asked, ignoring the ridiculous comment about men walking on the moon, and taking in the thin teal-blue silk dress Sage was still wearing.

Sage looked down at herself. "I should put my other clothes back on," and she left for the smaller room with Helen following. She pulled the wool pants up under the skirt of the dress, and began unlacing the bodice.

"Please keep the dress on; it looks so very pretty on you, better than it ever did on me, and it will be a way for Ethan to find us. He is coming with us, isn't he? He is very taken with you, you know."

"Yeah, I really like him too," she thought out loud. "I asked him to meet us on deck." Helen held the heavy wool jacket for her and Sage shrugged it on over the blue silk, relishing its warmth. The big ship shuddered.

"Right on time; it's 11:40."

"Was that...?"

"Yes, we just hit the iceberg. Here, put on this hat, and you'll need gloves too. The air is very cold tonight."

Then making sure Helen's coat pockets were deep enough to hold all the excess jewels *and* the napkin full of cookies, Sage strapped a life jacket on the young woman and ushered her out the door, up the stairwell, onto the deck, and into the cold night air.

"No one seems alarmed, Sage, is this a ruse?" Helen stopped defiantly.

"Most of the passengers don't realize yet what has happened.

They've been told the ship can't sink, and they believe it. For many, that stubbornness will cost them their lives. Even the crew will be slow to accept this fate. It won't take long though and the life boats will start to fill. This ship will be going down in two hours."

"Is that what has happened?" Ethan asked, coming up behind them. Sage smiled when she saw his heavy overcoat, muffler, and gloves.

"Oh, Ethan," Helen hugged him fiercely. "We've hit an iceberg, and the ship is going to sink!"

"We need to make sure Helen gets on that lifeboat," Sage said to Ethan and pointed to the large craft hanging by ropes and chains near the edge of the deck above the railings.

"What about you? Aren't you coming with me?" Helen asked.

"I told you, dear, I don't belong here. Once you're safe, I'll go home," Sage smiled sadly at her new friend. People then began to swarm out of the cabins and congregate around the lifeboats.

The captain stood on an upper deck with a megaphone. "It seems we have hit an iceberg, and it ripped a small hole in the starboard bulkhead. There is no need for alarm, however to be prudent, I'm asking everyone to put on a life jacket and prepare to board your assigned lifeboat."

"Too bad there aren't enough life boats for everyone!" Sage scowled.

"What do you mean?" Ethan asked, alarmed.

"There are only twenty boats, with a capacity for about eleven hundred people," Sage informed him.

"But there are over three thousand people aboard!" he protested.

"Which means a lot of people are going to die."

A steward came by handing out life jackets to those who didn't have one, and giving directions. "Once your jacket is on, please proceed to your assigned boat. We will board women and children first."

"Arnold!" Helen called out to the familiar steward.

"Ah, Lady Woodhaven, I'm pleased to see you have your jacket on. Are you ready to board? Miss Astor, Lord Woodhaven where are your jackets?" He roughly shoved two jackets at them. To avoid a confrontation, Sage let Ethan assist her getting one on.

The deck quickly filled with even more people trying to get to a life boat before it was lowered over the side.

Sage and Ethan took either side of Helen and helped her into life boat number eight. They stood by and assisted other women into the boat, including their portly tablemate who was brutal in her gossip of others. She looked positively and rightfully scared.

"Get that boat lowered!" A crew officer shouted.

"It isn't full yet," Arnold protested.

"Get it lowered, now!"

Life boat number eight began its descent. The stone at Sage's throat warmed slightly.

"You should have gotten on that boat, Sage!" Ethan protested. They both stumbled and swayed when the massive ship shifted and the deck tilted slightly.

"I'll catch the next one; Helen was the one to save." She looked at the handsome young man beside her, knowing he wouldn't be allowed into a life boat, and since she was still there something occurred to her. "Ethan, to settle my nerves, would you please look over the edge, and see if Helen is alright and that the boat is descending properly? I think if you step up on the railing, you can see more clearly." He did as she bid, a sudden wave of salty ocean water drenching them both.

"Yes, the boat is about ten feet down now." He let go of the railing and waved to his sister. Sage stood behind him and pushed, sending him overboard.

The stone grew very hot and she grew very dizzy. The life jacket dropped to the deck as she disappeared.

———— • ✷ • ————

"Sage!" Morgan called out. The girl lay in a heap in the center of the circles of flames. Morgan waved her hand, and the flames were gone. Only a few minutes had passed, yet Sage wore different clothes and seemed unnaturally disheveled.

CHAPTER NINE

———◦✦◦———

Morgan felt for Sage's pulse. It was strong and steady. The girl's physical body must be exhausted or in shock from the shift, she thought. Leaving the star stone around Sage's neck to help strengthen her system, Morgan lifted her staff, creating a three-way power surge, and levitated Sage off the floor.

Opening doors with a wave of her hand, Morgan also mentally sent the servants to another part of the massive house, and guided the energy force to take Sage up the stairs to her room where she could quietly and comfortably recover from the ordeal.

Once in Sage's room, she settled the girl on the massive bed and removed the star stone from around her neck. Morgan placed two fingers on Sage's forehead and said, "Sleep."

———◦✦◦———

"Lyle, can you and Jon come over at your earliest convenience? I have a matter I need assistance with that I feel the two of you would be perfect for," Morgan said the following day, mid-afternoon.

"My dear lady, we will be most delighted to help you in any manner. Do you need me to bring my swatch book?" Lyle answered.

Morgan laughed. "No, only your discretion."

An hour later a cab pulled under the portico, and the two men got out. The cab driver drove away without being paid. It was the same driver Morgan had used several times before, and he would be compensated another time.

"What can we do for you, Morgan?" Lyle asked. He and Jon had walked in, arm in arm, when Henry opened the massive front door and then led them to the library.

"It's about Sage," Morgan said. "Please, sit."

"I do hope the girl is alright! We both adore her!" Jon said, concerned, taking a seat beside Lyle.

"She will be fine. However, she's in a rather…exhausted state, and I need to get her out of her clothes, showered, and then into bed."

"And we being gay, make us your first choice?" Lyle said smiling.

"Darling, you two are always my first choice, for there is no one I trust more," Morgan stated honestly. "It's not only your discretion but your gentleness that I need and count on for this matter."

"Take us to her, Morgan," Jon answered solemnly.

⁕

"Oh, you put her in the peach room! How delightful," John clapped his hands quietly. Lyle had the taste of color and clothing fashion, and, while a cliché, his gay partner had the sense of color for interior decorating and had re-decorated Morgan's rooms a number of times.

Lyle gently gave his partner a stern look and Jon quieted.

Sage still lay as Morgan had left her twenty-four hours earlier.

"What will you have us do, Morgan?" Lyle asked.

"Sit her up and remove the jacket, then carefully take that dress off her, it's…quite old," Morgan thought, not knowing how something from the past would react to the time travel. Nothing was supposed to come back with her, yet this dress did for some reason. Under the dress was the pair of soft wool trousers, the suede shoes, socks, and underwear. As each item was removed, it was carefully folded and set aside or dropped into the laundry.

Morgan turned on the shower in the adjoining bathroom. "I will leave the two of you to figure out how to bathe her and get her back into bed. Meet me in the library when you are finished."

The two men looked at each other, shrugged, and began to undress. It would take both of them to hold the unconscious woman upright and get her cleaned up, and there was no need to ruin their own clothes in the process.

An hour later, Sage was back in bed, free of the salt spray in her hair, under the covers and sleeping peacefully. Her hair had been washed and dried, and she was left nude under the covers.

"And how is our patient?" Morgan asked, offering Lyle and Jon a glass of wine. Beside the bottle was a tray of various cheeses and crackers. She did note that their hair was damp yet their clothes were not and decided she didn't want to know the details.

"Sleeping like a baby," Lyle said affectionately, selecting a thin curl of soft asiago and let it sit on his tongue for a moment to savor the intense yet delicate flavor.

"What happened to her, Morgan?" Jon asked.

Morgan took a long drink of the white wine while she thought. "You two have been my best friends for over twenty years," she said.

"Yes, ever since you rescued us from that homophobic attack," Lyle shuddered.

"I never could tolerate intolerance," she said quietly then continued. "And you know who I am."

"Yes, you are a wonderful, kind, generous, beautiful lady...oh, and you're also a sorceress extraordinaire." Jon said matter-of-factly, munching on a freshly baked cracker.

Morgan smiled. "Sage just came back...from the *Titanic*."

"You did it? You sent someone back? Oh, how wonderful, Morgan! Congratulations!" Jon jumped up and hugged her.

"Don't congratulate me yet. I haven't spoken with her, so I don't know how it went," Morgan shrugged. "Because nothing has changed, I can only assume she was indeed the key to set into motion what would bring us to where we are now. I knew I made a good choice with her."

"When will she wake up?"

"I don't know. However if she doesn't come around by the morning, I will push the issue." Morgan stood to dismiss them.

"Would you like us here in the morning? Two extra familiar faces may be comforting to her, since she could be suffering some emotional whiplash," Lyle offered.

"I would appreciate that, thank you."

Sage woke the next morning from a timeless and mostly dreamless sleep, slightly disoriented. One minute she was standing on the deck of the *Titanic* as it was sinking, then she wasn't. Now she was in her bed, in her peach room and…nude. She frowned, wondering how that happened. That was some crazy dream she had. Her robe was on the deep-green padded chair beside the queen-sized bed like it always was. She slipped it on and went into the bathroom to take a quick shower. For some reason, she was incredibly hungry.

Refreshed by the hot water, Sage went to her closet, towel drying her short hair. She spotted the teal blue silk dress, and the towel slipped from her hands. It wasn't a dream. She stood there transfixed by the dress. Being a realist, she rationalized she must have had that dress before, and only never noticed it in all the beautiful clothes Lyle had selected for her. She pulled a pale-tangerine long-sleeved knit shirt over her head, added her brown trousers and, feeling a chill, slipped on the plaid wool jacket. She absently wondered where her dark green sweater was. With fur lined moccasins on her bare feet, she went in search of breakfast.

---- ❋ ----

"Oh, Sage, I'm glad to see you awake," Morgan greeted her. "I was afraid I would have to send Lyle to rouse you."

"Is there any breakfast left? I'm really hungry this morning!"

"I'm not surprised, you slept for two days," Morgan confirmed.

"Two days? Have I been ill? I had some weird dreams, although I don't remember much," Sage frowned.

"Sit, and someone will get you a platter." Morgan was concerned that she didn't remember her adventure.

With good timing, Lyle and Jon came in through the French doors from a walk in the domed gardens.

"There you are, our very own sleeping beauty," Jon said. They both kissed her cheek, and while Jon poured her some coffee and juice, Lyle went to the kitchen and filled a plate with eggs, bacon, and cinnamon toast and set it in front of her.

Once she finished the food, Sage leaned back and briefly closed her eyes. She looked at Morgan and said, "It wasn't a dream, was it?"

"No, it wasn't. Let's get comfortable in the library, and you can tell me all about what happened," Morgan internally breathed a sigh of relief: Sage didn't have a lack of memory; she was, however, in denial, at least she had been.

---- ❋ ----

"And then I pushed Ethan over the railing, hoping he would fall into the lifeboat and not the water. That's the last thing I remember," Sage finished her story.

"Wow, oh wow," Lyle leaned back in his chair. Jon had yet to say anything.

"And you said it would only be for a minute or two. I was gone thirty-six hours!" Sage exclaimed.

Morgan smiled. "It *was* only a few minutes here. Apparently, the star stone will keep you as long as you need to be gone. You did exactly what you needed to do to make this timeline turn out right."

"I don't understand. Wouldn't something have changed by my giving Helen all that information?" Sage was confused.

"I believe *now* happened because you *did* go back. You didn't change anything Sage, you *ensured* it would happen. This is wonderful," Morgan now smiled sadly.

"I'd like to know what happened after I…left," Sage frowned.

"That's simple. Helen told me the story so many times when she got old, I know it by heart," Morgan stood to refill her cup of coffee. "First of all, yes, Ethan fell into the lifeboat, on top of some fat woman that cushioned his landing. When the *Titanic* survivors finally reached New York, Humphrey Tuttle II was there waiting for them. As you suspected, he was a greedy old man, and the first thing he asked about was her dowry; he wasn't the least bit concerned about their ordeal. At your suggestion, Helen told him the jewels had been lost; he was furious and tore up the marriage contract in front of her and tossed it in the gutter, telling her he would never marry such a homely waif without her dowry. He stormed away, leaving her and Ethan stunned and alone in a strange city."

"Homely? Helen was a beautiful, young woman!" Sage protested.

"If what she looked like twenty years later was any indication, I would agree with you," Morgan confirmed. "So, with Humphrey gone, Ethan was her rock and told her he would find a job to support them. I remember how she laughed over that. Ethan was an English Lord like their father and had no marketable skills. Then she lifted her scarf and showed him the jewels. Of course, Ethan was delighted, and she told him what you had related to her.

"They found rooms that would accept the pound notes Ethan still had in his pocket from playing cards the night of the sinking. After that, he took one bracelet to a jeweler and sold it, getting more for it than he imagined possible. He bought them a brownstone in

Manhattan to live in and rented out half, creating a steady income. He sold another piece and invested in the market, according to Helen's suggestions, and they made a fortune.

"In 1917, Helen met Doctor Sidney Malone. He was much older than her, but he loved her dearly and was totally devoted to her."

Sage laughed, "I knew she would find the right man to marry!"

"Yes, they married, and she moved into this house with him, giving Ethan full ownership of the Brownstone. Sadly, in 1918, Doctor Malone died from the Spanish flu while trying to help others. Helen was heartbroken, and, once again, Ethan was there for her. He moved in here to look after her."

"He was a good man...and an excellent dancer," Sage grinned.

"Once again, she did as you instructed, and in 1929 systematically pulled ninety percent of her stocks out of the market and bought gold and more apartment buildings which Ethan managed. They did well and thrived in a very poor economy."

"So, you knew her? How did you meet?" Sage asked, enjoying the follow up story to her adventure. Knowing Helen and Ethan had survived and did well warmed her heart.

"It was 1932, a little over two years after the crash. I, of course, had lost everything, and although I could have used my power to keep my wealth, I was bored with life. I was contemplating rebuilding my fortune the old-fashioned way, by working at it slowly, or moving on to someplace new.

"Helen found me on a park bench, quite close to where I found you, Sage. All those years, she remembered what you said about doing a good deed, and that she would know *who* when the time came, and to 'go with the flow.' She had said that when she saw the star stone around my neck, she knew I was the one. Helen took me in here, and I never left. As she grew older, I aged myself so she wouldn't suspect I was...different." Morgan took a sip of her cold coffee and passed her hand over it to reheat. "It was quite the experience for me to not use my powers like I was accustomed to doing; however, it was the prudent thing to do."

"What about Ethan?" Sage asked quietly, remembering his kiss.

"Oh yes, Morgan, what about the handsome Ethan?" Jon said with a delightful grin.

"I never met Ethan. In 1932, a week before I met Helen, he went back to England to settle the estate when their father passed away. We never heard from him again, and that distressed Helen for the rest of her life," Morgan confessed, and got lost in a sad memory. She turned to Sage and said, "You, my dear, have brought us a mystery. I can't quite figure out how that lovely dress came back through time with you."

"I have a theory," Lyle said, interrupting. "As we were undressing you, Sage, I noticed that you had several layers on."

"It was cold!" she replied. "Wait! *You* undressed me?"

"Don't be so startled, dear one. Jon and I undressed *and* bathed you. Who else is a lovely naked *unconscious* woman safer with?"

Sage tilted her head at them. "Makes sense."

"Of course, it does but back to the dress. It was between layers of twenty-first century items, which might have been the cause of it staying with you. Your life jacket on the other hand, was the outer most layer and didn't come with you," Lyle explained to them.

"Then I have that beautiful dress because of this jacket," she smiled and slipped her hands into the pockets out of habit, looking for her lip balm. Her eyes widened. Out of one pocket, she withdrew the ruby necklace.

"Oh my, It is as stunning as you said it was…is…whatever," Jon stammered. "How did it get in your pocket?"

"I don't know. I was with Helen the entire time…except when I stepped into the hallway to talk with Ethan. She might have put it in my pocket then, or when she helped me put on the jacket. I bet it was when I made up the pouch of cookies!" Sage looked at

Morgan. "What am I going to do with this?" she held up the ornate and heavily jeweled necklace.

"Why ask me? It's now yours. Helen obviously wanted you to have it." Morgan sipped again at her hot coffee. "It seems we have come full circle with this timeline. I befriended you; you befriended Helen; Helen befriended me, so I could befriend you. Plus, she gave you one additional gift. You are now a wealthy woman, Sage. Oh, I almost forgot, while you were sleeping, I took the liberty of depositing your apartment refund into an account for you. Here is your new debit card." Morgan placed the small sliver of dark blue plastic in front of Sage.

"I think we should celebrate with a night on the town!" Lyle announced.

"Oh, yes!" agreed Jon. He turned to Sage. "This is really *your* celebration. Where would you like to go?"

"I'd like a pizza and wine—lots of wine," she said, slipping the debit card into her pocket.

"Then we shall start our evening with champagne!" Morgan was delighted to have Sage back, not only physically but mentally as well. It had concerned her greatly what the effects of time travel might have on the young woman. Her fears were unfounded; Sage had handled the transition better than expected.

The four friends sat at a small round table, covered with a traditional red and white checked cloth. In the very well-appointed hole-in-the-wall pizzeria, they laughed at each other's jokes and sipped dark-red zinfandel wine. The pizza was delivered quickly and sat in the center of the table, oozing perfectly melted cheese and loaded with everything except anchovies. Although the men liked the salty little fish, Sage did not, and since it was her party, it was left off. The delicious aromas almost made Sage swoon.

"And when Helen saw my lacy bra and panties, I thought she was going to faint from embarrassment!" Sage laughed, recalling the incident from what was to her only a few days ago, although in reality it was a century past.

"Oh, how did you explain that?" Jon asked, grinning.

"I told her it was a new Paris fashion," she said, much to everyone's amusement.

"That was quick thinking, Sage, however for your next...trip... perhaps I should do some research and clothe you more appropriately," Lyle suggested.

Sage went still, a folded piece of pizza half way to her mouth. "Next trip?" she set the slice back down on her plate and looked over at Morgan.

"We're not done yet, Sage, and Lyle is right, you need to be dressed more to the time in which you will appear," Morgan agreed. Seeing Sage's face fall into a frown, she added, "that won't be for some time yet. It's nothing to get concerned about." She reached out and touched Sage's hand tenderly, removing the worry from her mind. "Let's take the rest of this pizza home and finish it with more champagne!" Morgan suggested, standing.

Sage gladly paid the tab with her new debit card, while Morgan flagged down their taxi.

CHAPTER TEN

"**W**hen was the last time you were at the Smithsonian, Sage?" Morgan asked over morning coffee a few days later.

"I hate to admit this, but I've never had the time to go," she confessed sadly.

"Then that is what we will do this week," Morgan announced.

"This *week*?"

"My dear, the museum is so big it's impossible to see it all in one day. Each wing needs a full day to appreciate what is there," Morgan informed her. "Oh, this is going to be a delightful experience for you. Being a history major I'm surprised you haven't *created* the time."

"I found a job so quickly I rarely had any spare time. Thank you, Morgan. This is going to be a dream come true for me."

Me too, Morgan thought silently.

Morgan booked them into a lovely hotel across the way from the Smithsonian in Washington, D.C. a few days later, taking most of the early day to travel to the capitol.

They took the rest of the afternoon to admire the Jurassic period displays and dinosaur re-creations. The tunnel that had been turned into an Amazon-like forest was surprisingly empty. Sage lingered at the primordial swamp, breathing in the humidity and mossy scent while recorded animal calls sounded gently in the background.

"This is amazing, Morgan. Where are we going tomorrow?"

"How about Egypt? I hear they've recently completed building a replica of a tomb, one without all the traps and superstitions," she grinned. "And fortunately for us, the King Tut exhibit has been returned so we can see that too."

On the fourth day of their Smithsonian wanderings, Morgan insisted on visiting the American History wing.

"I was here many years ago and was totally captivated by the First Ladies exhibit. These are the actual dresses worn by the president's wives. The mannequins are not only dressed in the real clothes but also their shoes, gloves, whatever was salvaged and all of it is encased in airless glass cases to preserve the material," she explained while they walked around the large glassed in exhibit.

"Wow, they were really short!" Sage commented.

"Yes, they were, compared to today that is. Both Martha Washington and Mary Todd Lincoln were a little over five feet tall, whereas their husbands were over six feet tall. That was tall for a man though. The average height for men in the 1800's was five foot six," Morgan read from a mounted plaque in front of a display. Morgan lowered her voice and added, "I'm five foot five and was taller than most back then!"

"Huh, I'm five-seven. I guess I'd be considered tall back then, not now though." Sage stooped to look closer at the shoes. "Their feet were so tiny! This has been really interesting, Morgan."

"Anything else historical you would like to see?"

"Of course," Sage laughed. "I want to see the space exploration wing, and the inventions, and I think I'd like to go back to Egypt."

"Egypt has always captured my interest too. We'll come back another day for that. I'm afraid I'm getting tired with all the walking."

———— ✳ ————

"Alyce has come through again with an incredible meal," Sage said later in the evening after they returned home. "I never would have thought of broiling chunks of crab on top of a fillet mignon."

"That was delicious," Morgan stood in front of the blazing fireplace in the library. "Sage, are you ready for more travel?"

"You mean *time* travel, don't you?" Sage asked hesitantly. "Where, or rather when, are you thinking of? I'll be the first to admit this really makes me nervous."

Morgan turned to face her. "Sage, I've promised that no harm will come to you. Don't you trust me?"

"Yes, Morgan, I trust *you*, I don't trust the suddenness of the events. It's the not knowing where I am or what I'm supposed to do that got to me last time. What if I say the wrong thing and screw up someone's timeline? What if I cause someone to die or live, that should have lived or died? That weighs heavy on me."

"You did fine with the *Titanic*," Morgan reminded her.

"I was lucky."

"You trusted your instincts and they didn't let you down. That's what you need to keep doing."

"Go with the flow?" Sage said without smiling.

"Yes, dear, go with the flow, but think of what direction the flow is going; let the events unfold around you and see where it takes you." Morgan took her hand. "I searched a long time for you, Sage. It wasn't easy to find someone with your kind heart and your sense of fairness. Those are key to our success."

"So where are you going to send me? I hope not the *Lusitania*."

Morgan chuckled, "No, not there. You're going further back, a couple of generations further. I don't know what is there that awaits you, only the crystal stones know for sure, however that's where the stones say you must go. I am confident though that you will know when it presents itself and do the right thing." She hooked her arm with Sage's and walked them out of the library. "I need to discuss clothing with Lyle. The *Titanic* was recent enough that you were able to make do with the clothes you had, any further would have been…complicated." At the bottom of the stairs, they parted. "Get some rest, Sage; we have some work to do tomorrow."

CHAPTER ELEVEN

———————— ◆❋◆ ————————

"**A**nd what is *this*?" Sage protested, holding up a white linen pant-like garment with a ribbon at the waist.

"That is nineteenth century underwear, usually referred to as bloomers or pantaloons. The correct term is Pantalettes," Lyle explained. "You aren't going to get away with lacey undies this time, missy!"

Sage examined the soft material. "Wait a minute, this has a slit up the crotch!"

Lyle sighed and shook his head. "Yes it does, it's so you can lift your skirts and squat to pee. There are no padded toilet seats in the 1800's, only latrines and most of those were only a ditch that everyone used."

Sage went wide-eyed at the thought. "1800's? That was a really rough time..." She picked up the next garment. "Culottes?"

"Very good!" Lyle teased her. "Split skirts were very popular in the latter half of the previous century. They allowed women to move about more freely; to ride bicycles and especially to ride a horse." He picked up a long sleeved, high-necked blouse. "Be thankful I'm not asking you to wear a corset, which was still the fashion until the early 1900's when they gave way to bra's and girdles. Here, try this on," he handed her the blouse and a camisole top.

She stepped behind the folding screen to put the garments on, the bloomers and the split skirt. Lyle had scoffed at the screen but deferred to her modesty.

Emerging, Sage looked in the full-length mirror, smiled and said, "I look like a Gibson Girl!"

"Not exactly," Lyle casually said. "Gibson Girls were the epitome of femininity."

Sage was crushed and it showed.

"Oh, my dear, that wasn't an insult."

"Yes, it was," Morgan said from across the room where she'd been watching so silently they forgot she was there. "Apologize, Lyle." So rarely did she scold or reprimand Lyle, that it stunned him. He quickly remembered when she saved him and Jon from that gang: she was fierce and the aftermath was quite...messy.

"My deepest and sincerest apologies, Sage. I didn't mean it as an insult," he capitulated. "You see, Gibson Girls had hour-glass figures, piles of hair and were basically useless in society. You on the other hand, while your figure is quite pleasing, have very short hair and are far from useless."

"You're forgiven," Sage relented. "What do you think, Morgan?"

"You look like a schoolmarm, and that's exactly the look I want. Turn around please."

Sage turned slowly so Morgan could see her from all the angles.

"What else do you have, Lyle?"

"There is another skirt, a cloak and a bonnet. My thoughts are that she should wear all of them at the same time for...traveling." Lyle laid the brown and red striped skirt and darker brown cloak on the top edge of the modesty screen. "This is called a slat bonnet; it's an everyday sun bonnet and adjusts at the neck with the ribbons. It even folds flat when not worn," he explained, handing her the brown and red plaid hat. "And once again your shoe boots are classic in design and won't even be noticed."

"A bonnet would help hide her hair, at least temporarily. Sage, you need a new cover story for the short hair. Though I admit the story of burrs in your hair was ingenious. Remember, an illness wouldn't be good, not with all the sickness of that era." Sage nodded at her benefactor. "In wearing everything, it's assured a suitcase wouldn't get stolen somehow or lost. Think that one over too, Sage."

"A travel bag," Sage corrected and then slipped behind the screen, pulled the long skirt and petticoat over the split skirt, shouldered the cloak on and carried the bonnet out. In the mirror, she put the bonnet on and tied the ribbons under her chin and then turned to Morgan.

"What's the matter Sage? You look pensive," Morgan stated.

"I don't know if I can do this. The 1800s were a dangerous period of our history."

"And the *Titanic* wasn't?"

"To be completely honest here, I didn't believe you could really send me to another time and when you did, I had little choice but to…go with the flow or more like sink or swim."

"Since you know the history and what is to come, it will be safer for you, right?" Lyle chimed in.

"Just…go with your instincts again and you will be fine." Morgan stood and led them to her personal rooms. "This requires a great deal of my concentration, Lyle, so you can't come with us." He tipped his head in a slight nod and backed out of the room.

"We're going *now*?" Sage asked in a panic.

"Yes. You're all dressed for it and my energy is high. All the signs say now. I didn't say anything earlier because I didn't want to make you any more nervous than you were already." Morgan led the girl to the center of the room again, placed the serpent and the blue crystal stone around her neck, tucked it into the high collar, and began tracing the flames around her, chanting as she went. A final motion with the staff, and Sage disappeared.

CHAPTER TWELVE

———— ✦ ————

"**A**re you daft, woman? Get down!" someone yelled from behind her. Sage turned, confused, as a lead minié ball ripped through the sleeve of her blouse causing her to jerk and fall against the man behind her. Blood soon saturated her arm, and she fainted from intense pain.

"What in god's name is she doing in the trenches? Crazy woman, doesn't she know there's a war going on?" The sergeant easily picked her up over his shoulder and ran, crouching away from the shooting. He dropped her gently on the ground next to a wagon filled with wounded. He pulled a rag from his pocket and tied it around her arm.

"What's she doing out here?" the wagon driver asked, shaking his head.

"I don't know. I wonder if she's Doc Colter's new nurse?" the sergeant speculated. "I heard he had sent for one. Maybe you should get this load of wounded to Matthew, have him check her over, and then take her to Colter."

———— ✦ ————

Sage came to from being jostled around in the back of the wooden wagon. She looked around and saw wounded and bleeding men, most of them unconscious. A fresh wave of pain struck as her shoulder hit the wooden side boards, almost causing her to black out again. She fought the pain and searched for the source. A dirty, bloody rag was tied around her aching arm. Sage pulled at the loose knot and tossed the filthy material away. Fresh blood oozed down her sleeve when she tried to sit up straighter. Basic first aid crept into her thoughts: *staunch the bleeding*. She lifted her skirt slightly and ripped a long strip of material from her petticoat, wrapping it tightly around the wound. The wagon continued to bounce and jostle its cargo for several more painful minutes before coming to a halt.

"Matthew!" called out the driver. "Another load for you."

A short burly man stumbled out of the makeshift lean to and looked into the wagon. "What's this? You boys on the front having some entertainment you didn't tell me about?" He grinned devilishly at Sage, until he saw her bleeding arm. He helped her down from the wagon and led her toward the lean to.

"Be careful with her, Matthew, that's Doc Colter's new nurse!"

"If you're Colter's nurse, what the devil are you doing out here?" Matthew repeated what everyone else had said. He sat her on a stool beside a marred and bloody table.

"I got lost," Sage mumbled for lack of a better answer.

"Well, let me look at your arm, then I'll send you to town," Matthew offered. He ripped her sleeve open more to better see the wound and pulled the bandage off. "I wish all my patients had such minor gunshot wounds." He picked up a rag from the table, dipped it in water and was about to wipe the blood away.

"Wait!" Sage jumped up. "That's not clean."

"Listen ma'am, nothing is clean here, but I still need to see to stitch you up," and he came at her again with the wet cloth.

"What is this place?" she asked, stalling while she looked around and moved away from him.

"I see who is still alive, and who might live another day. The rest get buried out back. Now, sit down, please."

"This is the triage?"

"I don't know what that means but this is the first stop for the wounded, and I decide who goes home, who goes to the doc, and who gets buried."

"Whisky!" she pointed to the bottle on the back counter. He handed it to her, expecting her to take a drink; instead she poured it over her arm, and screamed. "My god that burns!"

"That was a waste of good whiskey!" Matthew growled, and he grabbed the bottle out of her hand and took a drink himself before putting it back on the shelf.

"Now the wound is clean and disinfected. Look if you want but you're not stitching *me* up!" she growled right back.

"A feisty one, you are. Doc Colter is going to have his hands full with you!" he laughed loudly. "It doesn't look like it needs sewing anyway. The bullet barely grazed you."

Sage tore another piece of cloth from her under skirt and allowed him to tie it around her arm. She then watched as Matthew sorted out the men in the wagon, most of them being dragged away for burial.

"Okay, Johnny, take the lady to Colter." He turned his back to her and reached for the whiskey bottle.

The driver, Johnny, let her off in the small town without a word and drove the team of horses away.

Sage stepped into the busy road and was promptly pushed aside and down. "Sorry, ma'am, you stepped right in front of that stage-coach! Are you alright?"

Sage shook off his hand and glared at him, then began brushing the dirt from her clothes, taking the time for a longer look at her surroundings. The road, although now dry and dusty, showed deep ruts from use during a recent rain. The buildings, if one could call them that, were clapboard structures, mostly showing the dingy brown of the wood with the occasional fading whitewash façade.

"My apologies, good sir, for requiring your intervention. It seems as though I'm rather lost," Sage quickly recovered. The man that had saved her from being run down, stood in front of her now, hands on his hips…wearing a dark-blue Union soldier uniform with the three stripes of a sergeant. The kepi hat on his head sat askew from the fall. Confirmation that she had landed in the middle of the Civil War!

"You must be the new nurse. The doc has been expecting your arrival and told us to watch for you. He wants to see you immediately," The young man straightened, trying to add to his short height. As tall as she was she looked him level in the eye.

"Then, please take me to him." She lifted her chin as she suspected a lady of means and education would do, and followed him down the rugged wooden walkway that was barely two planks wide. Sage was careful where she stepped, so she didn't trip on the unevenness; a broken arm or leg in this difficult year would only spell disaster.

The sergeant's quick strides took them to a building that was only slightly in better repair than the others and opened the door. A sign over the door said "hospital" in crude printing. Inside was a small vacant room with a writing desk and four straight-backed chairs that looked incredibly uncomfortable to Sage.

"Hey, doc! Your new nurse is here!" the sergeant called out.

A tall man emerged from a doorway that wafted unpleasant odors. Doctor Edward Colter stood six-foot-tall, towering over the young soldier. His longish blond hair was tied in a short queue at the nape of his neck with a strip of thin, dark brown leather. His dark-brown eyes took Sage in at a glance: her new, stylish clothing, that trim narrow waist, and skin so clear and smooth that he ached to touch it. He swallowed hard.

"Thank you, Nichols, you're dismissed." He studied Sage again, setting aside his instant attraction and letting his anger take its place. "You're late, and you're injured. I will tend to that after we're done. You were to be here days ago. Your tardiness has been most inconvenient." He turned his back on her and went through the same door he came from, leaving it slightly ajar.

"This is going to be interesting," Sage muttered to herself and sat in one of the waiting room chairs, smoothing her skirt. She crossed her ankles demurely and waited, taking the opportunity to think about the situation.

She was a historian, not a nurse. Sage tensed at the thought of being expected to do medical procedures. Granted she had watched hours of *House* and reruns of *Marcus Welby*, but that was modern medicine and television, not a real-life situation. Maybe all she would be required to do was change Band-Aids or add fresh Neosporin. *No*, she thought again. Neither of those existed in the 1860s. *I hope my basic first aid classes will be enough here.* Her thoughts were interrupted when the doctor came back through the door.

"What are you doing sitting there?" he demanded.

"Until such time as I am instructed to do otherwise, I will sit here and rest. It's been a very trying journey," Sage smiled tightly at him and then stood. "In fact, I would like to see my room so I may freshen up."

He stared at her speechless.

"And, Doctor Colter, it occurred to me while sitting here, that you don't even know my name," Sage gave him a slightly softer smile.

"Of course, I do. You're Abagail Pursane, and I thought you would be more professional," he huffed.

"Therein lays the error in your assumptions. My name is Sage Aster; Abagail was unable to accept the post, and I was sent in her stead." Sage felt a bit of smugness at her quick ingenuity.

"I see," the doctor muttered. "I will make do. Come with me,

there are patients to attend and surgery to perform." He turned toward the door again.

"And where may I wash my hands?" she persisted.

"Wash? What for?"

"Where may I wash, *doctor*?" she repeated, her voice stern. "I was pushed to the ground by the sergeant and my hands are filthy *and* bloody. I will not go near a patient with dirty hands!"

"Women!" he shook his head. "I will send Anna with a bowl and pitcher." He turned and stomped out.

A few minutes later a young black woman came through the door carrying a small ceramic bowl and balancing a pitcher of water in it.

"You sure have the doctor in a tizzy, miss!"

"You must be Anna. Thank you for bringing me some water to wash in. Can you also show me to my quarters? The doctor seems to have forgotten that small detail," Sage smiled at the pretty girl.

"Um, he didn't say nothin' about no room, miss."

"I will have to discuss that with him later, then." She removed her cloak and bonnet, setting them on one of the chairs.

Anna set the bowl and pitcher on the desk and stepped back while Sage rinsed as much dirt as possible from her hands and face. Looking around for a towel and not finding anything resembling one, Sage sighed and lifted the hem of her skirt and wiped her face. She was relieved that the bleeding had finally stopped. Her arm didn't hurt as much as it did before, and she guessed it was still numb from the dousing of alcohol.

"Your arm is bloody and wha...what happened to your hair, miss?" Anna gaped at her.

"I would rather not discuss that right now. Please take me to the doctor."

———⬩✳⬩———

Sage held her head high as she followed the girl through the doors and past several occupied beds. The stench was almost overwhelming, and her palms began to sweat. She wiped her hands on her skirt and felt a pocket. Reaching into the pocket she smiled, and removed a scented cloth hanky. *Thank you, Lyle*, she thought and held it over her nose to stem the rank odors.

The doctor was leaning over one of the beds adjusting a bandage when she arrived. Anna quickly left the room.

"I see you finally decided to make an appearance Miss Aster," he said gruffly. Looking up, he said, "What happened to your hair?"

Sage rolled her eyes. "If you were to give me five minutes of your time Doctor Colter, I would be happy to explain a few things to you about myself. Otherwise, you can continue to allow my appearance to distract you, or we can get to work."

"Re-bandage this patient's wound," he replied with a sneer.

She looked down at the boy on the bed. He couldn't be much more than sixteen or seventeen years old, she thought, and now would have to go through the rest of his life minus his left arm, which had been amputated at the elbow. She looked around and not seeing what she wanted, called out.

"Anna! Bring me a bowl of warm water and some clean bandages, please." Sage began removing the filthy and sticky pieces of cloth from what was left of the boy's arm.

Anna set the bowl of tepid water on the bed, and placed a few strips of dingy white cloth beside it. She looked away from the festering sores and stepped back, bumping into the doctor who was watching with interest.

"I also need a bucket or bowl to dump these…these rags in! And for god's sake open some windows in here, I can barely breathe!" Sage finished removing the old bandages, and gasped at the massive infection. Red lesions snaked up his arm and swollen skin split, seeping yellow and green pus. She glared at the doctor. "How did you let him get this infected?" she demanded, dipping a clean cloth into the water. Slowly she removed the caked-on seepage, exposing the dying flesh.

"I didn't *let* him get infected, Nurse Aster, he was already in this condition when he showed up this morning." Edward took the dirty bandages from the foot of the bed and dropped them into the wooden bucket Anna had brought. He continued to watch as Sage finished washing the horrific wound and bound it with fresh cloths. When she took the last one and tore in down the center, tied a knot to stop the tear, then wound it around securing the other bandages, he nodded in approval.

"Let's go to my office and talk, Miss Aster." Edward turned and walked away, while she followed silently.

Doctor Edward Colter sat behind his desk, head in hands, breathing in the cleaner air. He looked up at his new nurse. "Now, Miss Aster, tell me about yourself: Where are you from? Where did you go to school? And where did you learn to double loop those bandage ties? That was impressive. And how did you get injured, and what happened to your hair?"

Sage had been thinking about a cover story ever since she had arrived. Now was the time to see how believable it was. As a history major, she knew that the biggest killer during the war was the lack of sanitation and contaminated water, which allowed diseases to spread. Diseases like typhoid, measles, tuberculosis, malaria, and pneumonia were very common.

"So many questions. First of all, doctor, it is *Mrs.* Aster, I'm a widow. My short hair is the result of my stepdaughter having an angry conniption fit and cutting large pieces of my hair off while I slept. Fortunately, one of my servants has a talent for trimming hair, and she cut mine so it could grow back more evenly.

"My nursing training was at my husband's side. He was a good doctor; sadly, he succumbed to a lung infection which he described to me to be pneumonia. He believed it was the closed quarters of the hospital rooms which promoted the disease, and why I insisted on the open windows."

"Out of curiosity only, may I ask why your step-daughter was angry?" he asked cautiously. This woman was lovely, talented, and educated, and he could see a young girl being jealous but why angry. How she answered would tell him a great deal about his new nurse.

Think, Sage, think!

"Being her legal guardian now, I refused my permission for her to marry. She is only fourteen and her gentleman-friend is a ne'er-do-well. In time she will thank me, for now, I wear a lot of bonnets," Sage smiled.

Edward laughed.

"I sent for her aunt to stay with her while I came here. She is an unstable child, and I feared scissors in her hands may get closer than just my hair."

Edward's laugh turned to a shocked scowl.

"And, Doctor Colter, during my trip here, my travel bag was stolen. I have only what I'm wearing, which is most unsettling. It also means I have no funds to get a boarding house room and require housing here. And my injury is only a flesh wound from being dropped off at the front fighting line instead of here." *There, Sage thought, that should cover everything.*

"Of course. There are plenty of vacant rooms here. Anna will clean one for you."

"While on the subject of Anna, may I ask her...position here? Is she a servant or a slave?"

"I own no slaves, Mrs. Aster. Anna and her younger brother live here under my protection as house servants, along with Sara who does the laundry. There are other Negro servants as well that do the heavy work and the gardening. They too are under my protection. Mary is my cook, and you will rarely see her. She was badly burned in a fire that claimed her husband and son, and she is very self-conscious of the scars. After I did what I could for her injuries, she stayed on—it was that or live on the street and die there. All of them are housed and fed well. I can sense you will ask me sooner or later about them. They are not paid, except for my generosity. And they are free to leave whenever they wish, yet they stay," he replied. He stood, "And now, I believe we should get back to the work at hand."

"One final question, if I may," Sage stood also. "What is the function of this hospital?"

"This was once a hospital of healing and hope; it is now where the wounded and maimed soldiers come to die in comfort and peace."

"And what is your rate of...death?"

"Nearly one hundred percent," he answered in frustration.

"Perhaps we can improve those odds." *Was this her mission?*

CHAPTER THIRTEEN

———————•◦❈◦•———————

age took her cloak and bonnet to her recently cleaned, tiny
room, which consisted of a desk and chair, a clothing tree, and
a narrow bed. At least the bed had a little padding and a blanket. She hung the dark-brown cloak on the clothes tree and patted it
down. Lyle had surprised her by adding the handkerchief to her skirt
pocket, and she was hoping there were a few other goodies hidden
somewhere. She wasn't disappointed. In a nearly invisible pocket in
the lining of the cloak, she found a comb and a bar of lavender soap
cut into four pieces and wrapped in heavy paper.

"Lyle, I love you!" Sage whispered to herself, sniffing the fra-
grant soap. She set the soap and comb beside the basin and pitcher
of water. Anna had thoughtfully left two hand towels for her, and
Sage vowed to give the young girl at least one of the pieces of soap.
Perhaps she would give her all of them if she did whatever she was
supposed to do and went back to her own time quickly.

Sage took off the dark split skirt from underneath and hung it
up beside the cloak and bonnet. The full striped skirt was already
soiled and likely to get worse as the day progressed. At least in the
morning she would have something reasonably clean to wear. Her
blouse was a different matter.

———————•◦❈◦•———————

Sage made her way back to the infirmary determined to make a difference, even if it was a small one.

"Doctor Colter had to leave to deliver a baby on the Lubick farm outside of town, ma'am," Anna announced. "He told me you lost your baggage and to get you some extra clothing. I will set some things in your room later. He also said I was to help you in any manner. What would you like me to do?"

Sage looked around. "We're going to clean this place up. First, open more windows and get some air in here; perhaps smelling the fresh air will help to raise the patient's morale."

Anna and her younger brother, Joshua, scurried around to do her bidding, happy to have something different to do.

"Show me what you did with the dirty bandages from earlier." Sage knew that sterilization was unheard of, and she was hoping that introducing that concept would send her home.

"I try to wash them as best I can, ma'am," Anna said honestly, showing Sage the area used for washing everything. On the floor were two buckets, one filled with festering bandages, the other filled with cold dirty water. "Sara does the household laundry, and I do the bandages by rinsing them out two times."

"I see. We are going to make some changes in your method, not that it is wrong, only it could be better," Sage said. "The bucket with the bandages will be for the first stage of soaking." She picked up the bucket of dirty water and poured it over the pieces of cloth. Scabs and chunks of dead skin clung to the sides. "This bucket needs to be rinsed out really well and filled with clean water for the next rinsing. We will also require another container of boiling water that will stay on the stove."

Anna looked confused, but did as Sage said. Water was already heating on the massive wood cookstove so she moved it to a more accessible position.

Sage took a laundry stick and stirred the cloth bandages. She picked up a relatively clean piece with the stick and dropped it into the next bucket. After stirring it again, she lifted it from the second bucket and dropped it into the boiling water.

"This is the new method, Anna. Once all the bandages have been rinsed of the...the..." she so wanted to say *crap*, "disgusting pieces clinging to them and are in the clean water, they are rinsed again and put in the boiling water to kill any additional infection. While the water boils, the first bucket is emptied outside and rinsed of anything lingering. The water from the second bucket will now be used to soak the next batch of bandages, and fresh water is always used for the second rinse. Do you follow?"

"Yes, ma'am! I can do this," Anna smiled. "What do we do now?"

"Next this place needs to be swept and all the bedclothes need to be changed and washed," Sage instructed.

"We don't have enough to do them all at one time, ma'am," Anna protested.

"Then they will be done in shifts, a few at a time," she said and looked around at the vacant beds. "If those linens are clean, then there are four beds ready. We will move some of the men, and then wash those sheets."

"Sheets?"

"Bedclothes, I meant." *Careful Sage,* her tiny voice spoke in her head. "And we will continue moving the patients around until everyone has a clean bed. In fact, from the looks, and smell, of these men, *they* need to be washed also."

"Joshua, stoke the fire to heat more water," Anna commanded her brother.

"If we do this systematically, the men can be showered before they are put back into a clean bed," Sage announced triumphantly.

"Showered? Sheets? Forgive me, ma'am, you use words I never heard before," Anna said, looking down at her feet in embarrassment.

"A shower is something my husband designed so a person could wash in clean warm water that poured over them, much like standing in a warm rain. If you can find me some paper and a quill, I will draw it and perhaps one of the other servants can build it," Sage said. "In fact, is there a room nearby that is unused?" she questioned thoughtfully.

Anna led her to a door at the end of patient's dormitory. Inside was cluttered with broken furniture waiting to be repaired.

"This is perfect! It will be our new *rain room*," Sage grinned with glee. "Get a couple of the men to empty this room out quickly and then sweep it clean."

"Now right here," Sage made an X on the floor with a piece of coal, "cut a hole to let the water run down. Then nail down a four-foot square of timbers that will help keep the water contained in one spot." She showed the large servant what she meant, and he nodded.

"What will it be for, ma'am?" Anna asked.

"The patients will sit on a chair over this hole, and warm water will be slowly poured over their head so they can wash. The water will go down the hole to the ground underneath." She explained.

"Isn't that a waste of water?"

"Perhaps it may seem that way, but it's a way to wash the... sickness off the patients. The water will be full of that sickness and shouldn't be used for anything else."

Anna looked perplexed, but said she understood. "How will the water get on top of them?"

"Someone will have to pick up the bucket and pour it. It should be one of the men. It wouldn't be proper for one of us to be in the same room with a naked man," Sage explained.

"Naked?" Anna gasped. The other servants all stopped moving and stared.

"That's the only way to get their bodies clean, Anna. They need to remove their clothing for it to be washed anyway, so that would be a good time for them to be washed too."

"I dunno bout this, Anna. This new woman has some strange ideas," the tall man said, easily lifting two water buckets and taking them to the new room.

"Maybe she does, George, but they's good ideas. You know how good you feel when you put on clean clothes for Sunday church, why shouldn't these poor soldiers feel that too? They got hurt fighting to free the Negro slaves in the south. Besides, the doctor said to do anything she wants," Anna told him. "Now, Samuel will bring the first man into the room and help remove his clothing. While you help wash that poor soul, I'll wash his clothes. Now do what Misses Aster says, and we will be done in no time."

"What are we going to do, ma'am? The men might get washed but they clothes will still be wet," Anna said pacing.

"Stop your worry, Anna," Sage took the woman by the shoulders. "We have at least four towels, right? After the men wash and have dried with a towel, they wrap the towel around their middle in modesty and go back to their clean bed and cover up with the fresh bedclothes. No one will see their naked bodies. Once the first four men are back in their beds, I will come in and re-bandage their wounds. We may have to do the other four men tomorrow, though, unless we get a strong warm wind that will dry the sheets quickly." Sage found it difficult to call the sheets *bedclothes*, and was thankful Anna now understood what she meant.

With the first four men back in their clean beds and their bandages changed, Sage made her way to the laundry room to see how the next set of sheets were coming along.

"Ma'am?" a weak voice called out to her.

"Yes, soldier, what can I do for you?" She stopped and smiled at the young man. She knew his arm was so badly infected he likely wouldn't make it through the night.

"Forgive me ma'am, I can't help but see what you are trying to do for us and I want to thank you," he winced in pain. "When I was younger and worked on my daddy's farm, I remember during the summer, when work was done, I would go to the creek and sit in the shallows. The cool water would wash away all the dirt and sweat, and it would feel so good I almost hated putting back on my dirty britches." He coughed. "I know I'm dying, ma'am, and I don't want to die filthy like this. Please, can I bathe next?"

Sage stifled a sob. "Absolutely. What is your name?"

"Alfred, ma'am, Alfred Beals, and thank you."

"Let me help you up, Alfred. I'm sure there is some warm water ready." Sage held the young man's good arm and led him to the new rain room. With the servant men watching, Sage tenderly removed the man's shirt and then very carefully unwound his bandages. "I will now leave you in the care of these gentle, nice men, Alfred. When you're washed and in bed again, I will be back." She smiled and left the room.

Outside the room, the tears rolled down her cheeks.

"Miss Sage? What's the matter?" Anna questioned softly.

"I'll be fine. We need to change the bedclothes on bed number six immediately."

"There aren't any dry...sheets, ma'am," Anna said, proud to have added a new word to her vocabulary.

"Then take them off *my* bed. That man *will* have a clean bed tonight!" Sage shoved open the door near the kitchen which lead to the outside. Once in the warm afternoon air, she hung her head and sobbed. "I can't do this, Morgan!" *Yes, you can, because you have no choice,* her conscience said.

CHAPTER FOURTEEN

---·◦·◉·◦·---

octor Edward Colter returned to his hospital the next afternoon. Exhausted and depressed, he dropped his heavy overcoat onto the nearest chair and walked into the patient dormitory. The change was immediately obvious.

Sage closed the book she was reading aloud and stood. "Welcome back Doctor Colter. Would you like a progress report?" She smiled innocently and followed him out.

"What have you been doing?" he bellowed, sitting down. "This is not a hotel!" He seemed to be unnaturally agitated with her.

"No one is more aware of that than I am, doctor. However, you yourself said these men come here to die in comfort and peace, I've added dignity to that. They have clean beds, clean clothes, clean bodies and clean dressings for their wounds. They are at peace with themselves now, and some of them just might survive." Sage finally sat. "How was the delivery?" she changed the subject without hesitation.

He glared at her momentarily, then leaned back in his chair and closed his eyes. "It was a breach birth. Both mother and infant are alive—for now. There wasn't anything further I could do." He reached into a drawer and brought out a full bottle of whiskey and a glass, poured a shot and downed it, poured another. "So, tell me what you've done to bring these poor sots dignity?"

81

"It's been quite simple, doctor, as I said I offered them cleanliness. Cleanliness reduces the chance of further infection and helps to heal what is already there…unless it's too far gone." Sage swallowed hard. "Alfred Beals died this morning."

"Who?"

"The young man that came in a few days ago with half his arm amputated. As you say, there was nothing further I could do."

"I heard you reading to the men. I didn't know you could read."

"I can read *and* write, doctor. I was university educated. Alfred asked me to read to him, so I did. The other men enjoyed it and asked me to continue, so I did. By reading them only one chapter at a time and not finishing the story, they have the incentive to live another day to hear more—Scheherazade in reverse."

"What or who is Scheherazade, and what pray-tell were you reading?" His voice softened in exhaustion.

"I was reading Journey to the Center of the Earth by Jules Verne," she replied, skipping an explanation about Scheherazade.

"Humph…rubbish," he slurred.

"It was from *your* library, Edward," Sage snickered. Noticing that he was now snoring lightly, she draped a small couch blanket across him and let herself out to help Anna with feeding the remaining patients.

Alone in her room that night, Sage wondered what else she needed to do or who she needed to help, so she could go home. She had been in 1863 for three days, and it felt like forever. Her arm still ached, and she was always hungry. She hung her skirt and borrowed shirt on the coat tree and pulled a nightgown over her head. Anna had graciously washed and repaired her damaged blouse and had loaned her a few articles of clothing; the shirt fit well, however the nightgown caught her mid-calf since Sage was much taller than the servant girl. It didn't matter. Sage slept soundly every night from exhaustion, and the days passed in a blur.

"I can't do that, George! I can't walk, I'm missing a leg in case you haven't noticed!" one of the patients yelled.

"What's the problem here?" Sage asked sweetly to defuse any hostility.

"I apologize for yelling, ma'am, George here wants me to get into that chair by myself, and I can't even stand!" Johnny Allen said.

"What about the crutches you were given?" she asked.

"They hurt my underarms somethin' fierce."

"I see. You just lay there for now. George, come with me."

"I know we can't grow that man a new leg, Doctor Coulter, but maybe we can *make* him a new one," Sage said. "George has done some wonderful woodworking and is willing to try, however he won't without your consent."

"George, do whatever Mrs. Aster suggests. Anything to keep these men quiet." Coulter put his head back down on his folded arms. He thought it was the worst hangover he had ever had. Yesterday he got word both mother and infant Lubick had died.

Sage showed George the design she had drawn, a simple peg-leg with a wider top. "Now, if you can get some leather or other heavy cloth, we can fashion a cuff that will fit over his leg stump, and it will be either laced up or buckled—whatever works better. Make it a bit longer than needed, and we'll trim it down to fit his height."

George looked at the drawing wide eyed. "Yes, ma'am. I can make this. Will it really help him?"

"We have to try George. It will be up to him whether or not it helps."

The next morning George proudly took the new wooden leg to Sage.

"This is great. Thank you, George. Now, I need one more thing. It will look like two hitching posts, side by side, wide enough for a man to easily walk through," Sage thought of the therapy bars she had seen on TV.

"What's it for, Miss Sage?"

"Walking with a new leg won't be easy to begin with, and this will give support while they learn how," she answered. "Let's fit this on Johnny first so you can trim it if necessary."

That afternoon Johnny was hobbling around on his new leg, using the parallel bars to steady his movement. When he walked back to his bed by himself, the other patients applauded.

Doctor Coulter watched from the doorway, impressed with the young man's quick progress.

"It's his desire to move about on his own. Independence is a great motivator," Sage explained. *But I'm still here*, she thought.

"I think your encouragement helps a great deal too, Mrs. Aster," Edward said, smiling warmly at her.

"Johnny, your remarkable progress reminds me of a story," Sage said to everyone in the room. "A man walked into a pub and ordered a pint of ale. He looked around and noticed a sailor with a peg leg, a hook instead of a hand, and a patch over one eye. He finished his ale and said, "Sir, if I may ask, how did you come by a peg leg?""

"The sailor said," Sage changed her voice, "Argh, I was on the deck of me ship one day and the waves were rough and I was thrown overboard. Before I could climb up the rope ladder, a shark came by and bit me leg off! And that's how I got me peg leg."

"The other man bought a round of ale and said: what a story! How did you come by a hook for a hand?"

"The sailor said," she changed her voice again, "Argh, I was on the deck of me ship one day, fighting off a pirate ship, and as the last bloke left, he cut me hand off! That's how I got me hook."

"The other man said: I have to know the rest, sir. How did you come by the patch over your eye?"

"The sailor said," she altered her voice one more time, "Argh, I was on the deck of me ship one day, and a bird flew by and pooped in me eye."

"That's it? The other man said: a bird pooped in your eye?" She paused and looked around the room.

"Well, it was me first day with me new hook," Sage finished. The room was momentarily silent, until the doctor started laughing, and then everyone was laughing.

Edward looked around at the men and thought that was the first time he could recall hearing laughter in the hospital.

George was given a full-time job making new limbs for their patients, and Sage tried coming up with new jokes.

"What you've done has made an astounding change in the patients, Mrs. Aster," Doctor Colter said during their morning meal. "I am thoroughly impressed. Show me more of what you've done. Anything is an improvement."

Sage explained about keeping things clean, and how Anna was now sterilizing the bandages, which seemed to make the biggest difference—that and their attitude.

"Now I understand why you felt it necessary to wash your hands when you first arrived," he observed. "Is there anything you feel I should be doing as well?"

"Although I acknowledge the surgery is your domain, doctor, I did take it upon myself to…clean up in there while you were gone. Your surgical tools are now clean and ready for use. I've instructed Anna on how to do this properly, so she can do this…if I'm not available." Sage caught herself from saying "after she was gone."

"As gruff as I may seem, Mrs. Aster, I relish new techniques that may improve my doctoring skills," he smiled at her. "Would you do me the pleasure of dining with me tonight? Mary really is a very good cook, although lately all she's been called on to do is make soup or stew for the patients. I would very much like to hear more of your husband's innovations."

"I would be delighted to join you for dinner, and since we will be working closely, please call me Sage…Edward." She stifled the urge to say something about the chauvinistic comment that all she was doing were ideas from her *nonexistent* husband.

Dinner was rabbit stew, with carrots, turnips and potatoes from the garden the servants tended plus fresh baked bread and a pitcher of ale.

"When the war started, the garden was constantly being raided, so I had the men move it closer to the building," Edward explained. "Although it doesn't do as well in the new location, at least we get to keep it all."

"Maybe it only needs more sunlight. Plants, like people, thrive better with the sun," Sage smiled at him, and sipped at the beer that was served with the meal.

"You don't care for the ale?"

"It tastes fine, Edward. I do prefer wine with my evening meal though, and water or juice with the morning meal." As she said that, another thought occurred to her. "Where does the drinking water come from?"

"From the same creek all the water comes from. We don't drink much of the water as it tastes foul and often will make one sick," he said.

"Ah. You've seen how Anna now cleans the bandages by boiling them? If you boil fresh water the same way, the germs will be killed and the water won't make one sick." Was this it? She thought. Was this my ticket home?

"Wouldn't the water be too hot to drink then? And what are germs?"

She laughed lightly and avoided answering her slip about germs, which wouldn't be widely known about for almost two decades, "It must be cooled first of course. It does need to be kept separate from the other water, too. I wouldn't want to get it mixed up."

"You are a most intriguing woman, Mrs. Sage Aster, and most certainly the most intelligent woman I've ever encountered, and so beautiful." Edward looked at her as though he was seeing her for the first time. "I know I sent for a nurse for the duration of the war, however...I...I would like you to consider staying on here." He covered her hand with his own and a longing reached his chocolate eyes.

Sage smiled, thinking and feeling, there was something familiar about Edward.

On the fifth evening they shared the evening meal, Edward walked Sage to her room. She noted to herself that he had changed a great deal from their first encounter over a week ago. He was actually a warm and kind person, and she was beginning to care deeply about him.

"Rest well, Sage," he said, and leaned in toward her, pressing his lips against hers. She responded immediately and took comfort in how good his arms felt around her.

"I think I could get accustomed to that," he said with a lopsided grin. He ran his finger along golden serpent and touched the blue crystal at her throat, a strange look appeared in his eyes that faded quickly.

"I will see you in the morning, Mrs. Aster." Edward turned back to his own rooms, leaving Sage stunned and tempted to follow him. However, knowing morals of her time were vastly different than his, she did not.

The following morning, Sage felt itchy and could smell her own body odor. She pulled her cloak over the nightgown, put a piece of soap in the pocket, and padded down the stairs bare foot to find Anna.

"Is there hot water yet?" Sage asked. "I really want to take a shower before anyone wakes," She explained.

"Yes, ma'am there is hot water, but you can't let those men see you without any clothing on! They may be servants, but they still men!" Anna gasped.

"I can do this myself by dipping water out of the buckets with a cup. I need you to watch the door so no one comes in while I'm bathing," Sage explained.

Sitting on the bathing chair, Sage wet her hair down and soaped it with the chunk of soap from her pocket. Cup after cup, she rinsed her hair squeaky clean. She used a cloth wrapped around the piece of soap and lathered her body, carefully rinsing as she went. There was a half bucket left of warm water, so she stood and poured it over her head and sighed.

After drying her body as best she could, she finger combed her short hair, and then put the nightgown back on and stepped out.

"Oh, my, misses, you smell nice," Anna smiled. "And your clothes from yesterday are dry now, hanging next to the stove in the laundry space." She gazed at the now exposed necklace. "What a beautiful piece of jewelry, ma'am, and the chain is so detailed it looks almost alive."

"Thank you, Anna, the necklace is very dear to me." Sage felt the enchanted serpent purr. "There is a piece of lavender soap wrapped in a cloth for you on the bathing chair. I will get dressed next to the stove, so I don't catch a chill."

Anna scurried into the rain room to find her gift while Sage went to find her recently washed clothes. She stepped into the warm room and quickly dressed.

Seated at the writing desk later, Sage was surprised when a very young girl opened the door and stepped in. Sage guessed her to be no more than five years old, clothed in a dirty and ill-fitting dress.

"Are you the doctor?" the little girl asked in a squeaky tiny voice.

"No, I'm his nurse. Is there something I can help you with?" Sage asked gently.

"My doll needs surgery. Her leg fell off and everyone around town says the doctor is giving the men new legs and I hope he can give Sally a new leg, too," she held her doll in her arms like a baby.

"May I see Sally? I would like to examine her first so we know how much surgery she is going to need," Sage smiled and held out her hand. "What's your name?"

"Beatrice. Do you think you can fix her?" Beatrice put the doll in Sage's hand, and then handed her the detached leg.

"Well, now, I think you brought her to me just in time," Sage set the doll and leg on the desk, and rummaged through the drawers for a needle and thread. She made small careful stitches and reattached the torn limb.

"Thank you, Mrs. Doctor!" Sarah took the doll and ran out the door.

Edward Coulter watched the entire episode from a half-closed door, thinking what a wonderful mother Sage would make.

Two days later, little Beatrice poked her head in the door again, and, not seeing Sage, sat down in one of the hard wooden chairs to wait.

Edward was surprised to see the little girl when he passed through the waiting room. "Can I help you?"

"No thank you, sir. I'm waiting for Mrs. Doctor so she can fix Sally's other leg," the little girl answered with a smile.

"I see. How did Sally hurt her leg this time?"

Beatrice got a solemn look on her face and didn't answer.

"Beatrice, how did Sally hurt her leg?" Edward pushed.

Without looking up, she sniffled and then barely above a whisper said. "Father's wife doesn't like her. She doesn't like me either."

Edward went still. "Does your father's wife ever hurt you?" he finally said.

"Sometimes," she said quietly, "she says it's because I'm bad. I don't think I am, but she says I am. Please don't tell her I told you, please. She'll hurt Sally even more, and I don't want that."

Sage had been listening to the exchange from the other side of the partially opened door. She stepped in and smiled at the little girl.

"Good morning, Beatrice! Has Sally had another accident?"

Beatrice jumped up and ran to Sage. "Yes, she has. Can you fix her again?"

"I will certainly try." Sage got the needle and thread out again and sat at the small desk to sew, giving Edward a look signaling him to stay quiet. "So tell me, Beatrice, where is your father?"

"He went to fight in the war. He said it was his...duty."

"And where is your mother? Your real mother?" Sage asked, barely looking up from the sewing, giving the girl some time and space to feel safe.

"Father said she went to stay in heaven, and then he brought Tabitha to stay and said she was my new mother. Only, she doesn't want to be my mother. She wants her own babies not me. Maybe that's why she hurts Sally; Sally is my baby. I hope she doesn't hurt her babies like she does Sally."

Sage's heart hurt listening to the little girl's story. "There, Sally is all better now." She handed the doll back to Beatrice. "If Tabitha hurts Sally again, I want you to come back here right away. Okay? Promise?"

"I promise. Thank you, Mrs. Doctor!" and she ran out the door.

"Edward, that little girl's stepmother is abusing her! Is there a way we can intervene?" Sage glared at the doctor.

"What would you have me do?"

"I don't know, but abusive parents don't stop, and the beatings only get worse. One day that child will have *accidently* fallen down the stairs and broken her neck, or *accidently* tripped in front of a team of horses and been crushed, or *accidently* fallen in the river and drowned!" Sage paced the small waiting room.

Edward pulled Sage into his arms to quiet and comfort her.

"Edward, if anything else happens to that little girl, please tell me we'll take her away from that horrid stepmother."

The following morning, the little girl was back. This time both of Sally's arms had been pulled off, and Beatrice herself was moving very slowly.

"I'll fix Sally after the doctor and I have a look at you, okay?" Sage said softly. She took her into the small exam room that Edward used for patients other than the soldiers and had her sit.

"Edward! Beatrice is back and she's hurt, please come and take a look at her," Sage pleaded.

Sage undid the small buttons down the back of the girl's dirty dress. She lowered the top slightly and exposed massive bruises on the girl's back and arms. She and Edward both gasped at the sight.

"Sweetie, tell us what happened. I promise no one will hurt you again."

The child looked up through tear spiked eyelashes. "Tabitha was mad that Sally was all better again, and she beat me with a piece of firewood. Then she pulled at my arm real hard. When my arm wouldn't come off she took Sally and pulled off both of her arms."

"Where do you live, Beatrice?" Sage asked.

"I know where she lives," Edward finally spoke. "You two stay here." And he left with George.

An hour later they returned carrying two small bundles.

"I've given all of the girl's clothing to Sara to wash and repair," Edward said to Sage. "When we got there that woman was ripping up all of the girl's clothing! I think we've now turned into an orphanage too."

Anna cleaned the room next to Sage, and Beatrice moved in. And still Sage remained.

Another three days went by; therapy with the amputees was going well, men were surviving instead of dying and yet Sage was still there. Again, early in the morning she took her soap and went in search of a shower.

"I thought you might want some warm water, Miss Sage, so

it's ready for you," Anna said, "and your clothes are hanging by the stove all dry."

Sage washed quickly and with only her short nightgown on, went to the laundry to get her dry clothes. When she stepped in she sensed something wrong. Suddenly someone tossed a rough blanket over her head and picked her up over his shoulder. She didn't even have time to scream for help when they were out the door into the cool predawn morning. She had been kidnapped!

CHAPTER FIFTEEN

———————❋———————

Two hours later, Sage was unceremoniously dropped on a hard, dirty wooden floor. She struggled out of the blanket and got to her bare feet.

"What is the meaning of this?" she demanded and pulled the rough blanket tight around her shoulders.

"Save your protests, Mrs. Aster, and sit in that chair," a blond-haired man pointed with his quill and went back to writing. When he was done, he looked at her. "It's come to my attention that you have been aiding a Union doctor and have had some remarkable results."

"What of it?"

"I want to know what you are doing that is so different that it saves lives."

She glared at him. "Why should I tell you?"

"You are a nurse; I'm a doctor; we have both taken oaths to do our best to heal whenever possible, and you have knowledge I need!" he slammed his hand to the table.

"You could have asked instead of kidnapping me!" she retorted.

"Would you really have willingly come behind enemy lines to practice your profession, Mrs. Aster?" he said smugly.

"Enemy lines? Where am I?" Alarm laced her question. "Who are you, and how do know my name?"

"I'm Doctor Kyle Provost of the Confederate Army. I have a very reliable spy in Cadbury, Mrs. Aster, and they have told me all about you. And in case your geography knowledge is lacking, Cadbury is barely ten miles from the front lines of this war, and *we* are only one mile behind that fighting, and we *stay* one mile behind as we push forward."

Cadbury, I've never heard of the town, Sage thought. It must be one of those temporary towns that sprang up around the fighting.

"If you show me your surgery and recovery area I will tell you what you are doing wrong," she scowled. "*First*, I need shoes or slippers of some kind and a coat or cloak to cover myself. Your man took me before I could dress proper, and I would like something to eat and drink," Sage made her demands and stayed seated.

"Henry!" Doctor Provost called out. Within moments a young Negro boy hurried into the room. "Look at her feet, and find some shoes to fit!" The boy scurried away.

"While the boy is attempting to find you some footwear, tell me what you did at Edward's hospital."

"You know Doctor Colter?" she questioned.

"We were friends for many years—before the war that is." Doctor Provost seemed sad for a moment, Sage thought. "What did you do while you were there?"

"I cleaned up the hospital, and then I cleaned up the patients."

"How many have died this past week?"

"One."

"One? That's it?" He leaned back in his chair. "That's remarkable."

Henry silently crept into the room and placed a pair of shoes on the floor in front of Sage and backed away.

She slid her feet into the cloth and leather shoes. "Thank you, Henry. They fit well."

"You don't thank him, he's a slave," Doctor Provost said harshly.

"He's a *person!*" she retorted in anger.

He scowled at her and stood. "Come with me." He left the room, and, knowing she had little choice, Sage followed.

* * *

"This is the surgery," Doctor Provost said.

"Surgery? This looks like a slaughter house!" Sage looked around, wide eyed. "Don't you ever wash away the blood?"

"What for, there will just be more in another hour."

"Things need to be cleaner if your patients have any chance of surviving, Doctor Provost." She walked over to a make-shift table and saw his tools: dirty scalpels, blood and bone encrusted saws, plus other items she didn't have a clue what they would be used for. "The first thing you are going to do is wash these instruments! Henry!" she called out and the boy appeared. "Bring me three buckets of water, two cold and one hot."

"Don't order my slaves around!" he replied angrily.

"You want my help? Then shut up and *pay attention!*" Sage took one of the buckets of cold water Henry had set on the floor, and dropped all the surgical tools into the water to soak. She poured half the other bucket over the surgery table and started scrubbing it with a blood-stained towel. After dumping the rest of the cold water on the table and wiping it off, she poured the bucket of hot water and let it stand. "More hot water, Henry, please." She glanced at the arrogant doctor and dared him to oppose her being polite to the boy. Provost stayed silent.

Sage took the surgical instruments out of the cold water, one at a time, and scrubbed off anything stuck. When Henry brought the next bucket of hot water, she placed all the freshly washed instruments in the bucket. She looked at Provost, and said, "Your tools stay in the water until you need to use them, and after, they go back into a bucket of water to wash off the blood."

96

"I don't understand what good that does, Mrs. Aster," he said, confused.

"The men are sick, and the sickness—the infection—is in their blood. If you don't wash the tools, all you're doing is giving the next man the same infection," she knew she was losing her patience, but it didn't seem to matter.

"Doubtful that will help our next patient. He's in the other room waiting."

"What is the problem with him?" Sage asked hesitantly.

"He has blood poisoning, third case this week. I had to amputate the infected arms on the other two, and he's next."

A young man lay on the single cot; beads of sweat outlined his forehead and drenched his dark hair. His gray eyes followed the two people who entered the room.

"This man didn't last long in the fighting. He came in less than two weeks ago, and can't shoot worth a damn," Doctor Provost said to Sage. He pushed up the long sleeves with a stick of wood and exposed lines of red running from wrist to elbow.

"Where is the injury of origin?" Sage asked.

"That is the perplexing part of this: there is no injury," Doctor Provost said, his mouth pulled into a straight line of frustration.

Sage pulled up a chair and sat down next to the patient and smiled at him. "I'm going to look at your arm, soldier." She folded the sleeve back and pushed it higher.

"Please don't call me soldier. I didn't come here to fight. I'm a merchant and I was bringing supplies," he whimpered. "I was attacked by the Rebels; they took my horse and wagon and made me put on a confederate coat and told me to shoot anyone in a blue coat."

Sage frowned and idly scratched the back of her hand. She

looked closer at the red lines that were everywhere on his arm. She started to scratch her hand again and stopped.

"Have Henry bring two more buckets of cold water! And more clean rags." She turned to the man on the cot. "Take off your shirt and drop it on the floor." She plunged her hands into the fresh bucket of cold water and rubbed them together. She took one of the rags, wetting it with the water, proceeded to wipe down the man's arms. "If you look closely at these lines, doctor, you can see tiny tears in the skin. These are scratch marks, not blood poisoning tracks." She looked at the patient. "How long have your arms been itching?"

"Over a week now. What's wrong with me? It can't be the ivy, I haven't touched any, honest."

Sage looked up at the doctor. "If there have been others, I would say you have a saboteur in your midst. My guess is this man's shirt has an itching powder of some sort on it likely from the coat he was given. My hands started itching almost immediately after I touched the sleeves. Washing his shirt should take care of it." She dipped a fresh cloth into the cold water and pressed it to the man's arm. "This minor infection should heal on its own with some willow bark tea."

"Oh, that feels good," he sighed.

"Why would someone do that?" the doctor asked.

"Think about it. A soldier on the front lines is so distracted scratching, he is useless in shooting, or he gets injured. Then something like this happens and the scratches are easily mistaken for something else, and the soldier is then permanently maimed and sent home."

"That's…diabolical!" the doctor exclaimed, and started pacing.

"What's your name?" she asked the young man, smiling. Had she not been here, he would have had his life ruined by having one or both arms cut off in error.

"Humphrey, ma'am. Humphrey Tuttle."

Sage's eyes went wide with recognition, and the blue crystal stone grew very hot.

"Go home, Humphrey. Go home, get married, and have a son." She smiled and disappeared. Her borrowed clothes fell in a heap on the floor.

CHAPTER SIXTEEN

————•◦❈◦•————

Morgan was startled when Sage appeared in the circle only a few minutes after she had left. Sage swooned and crumpled, naked, to the floor. Morgan quickly doused the flames and rushed to her side. She snapped her fingers, and a large, soft blanket appeared. She covered Sage with it and stepped back. She held her hands over the unconscious girl and flickers of blue light emanated from her palms. She raised her hands, lifting Sage off the cold wooden floor.

Morgan walked with the levitated girl out the doors, mentally opening and closing them. In the hallway, Lyle was still waiting. He stood sharply at the sight and gasped, yet stayed silent. He wordlessly followed Morgan up the carpeted stairs to Sage's suite. When the three were inside the peach walls, Lyle stepped around the concentrating Morgan and tugged the bed covers back so the sorceress could lay Sage down. He pulled the covers over her slender naked body and stepped away to watch.

Morgan laid a cool hand across Sage's forehead, another under her chin and chanted an ancient language. She rested a hand on the healing wound near her shoulder, blue light pulsed bright and dimmed, and the ugly bruise was no more. Sage's fair skin had been restored.

Morgan lowered her head and breathed deeply. When she turned, she was surprised to see Lyle sitting in a chair by the door.

"She'll be alright, won't she?" he asked softly.

"Yes," Morgan said, and walked past him and out the door. "She's exhausted," she continued, knowing Lyle would follow her.

"How long will she sleep?"

"I don't know. As before, if she doesn't waken on her own within forty-eight hours, I will bring her around. However, this trip seems to have been emotionally traumatic for some reason and she had a partially healed gunshot wound on her upper arm."

"Partially healed? She was only gone a few minutes."

"From these two trips, it would appear that she comes back close to the same time she left, regardless of how long she spends in the past. I am concerned that her lack of clothing has something to do with the trauma," Morgan frowned at the thought.

Lyle grinned. "I don't think so. I could smell lavender when I covered her with the blanket. She had recently had a bath."

Morgan raised her eyebrows, looking at him in askance.

"I slipped her three things: a handkerchief, a comb, and some lavender soap." He giggled. "Nothing that would cause a stir if left behind, only things that could make her time in the past a little easier."

"What kind of comb?" Morgan asked solemnly.

"Just a cheap pl...astic one...oops."

"Don't do that again, Lyle," Morgan admonished him.

"I promise." He looked contrite. "May I stay until she wakes?"

"Lyle, my dear boy, you can stay as long as you want. I've told you before, that you and Jon could move in here if you so desired." Morgan had made that offer at least once a year over their twenty-year friendship, and she meant it more each time. She was powerful, and she was also lonely.

———————⊕———————

Forty-six hours after her abrupt return, Sage woke. As all the mornings while in the past, she reached for the assurance of the star stone. With it missing, she sat up in a panic to search for it. Realizing she was back in her own bed, in her own time, she laid back down in relief for a few seconds.

Sage took a quick, hot shower. After relishing the hot needle spray for an extra minute, she dressed in warm casual slacks, a fitted sweater and went in search of food. She was famished as usual.

In the greeting room, she had hoped to find the side-boards filled with food. The tables were empty. In the kitchen, she found Alyce kneading bread.

"Oh, my dear, what can I get for you? Miss Morgan said you were ill and not to be disturbed," Alyce said.

"I'm better now. I'd like some bacon and eggs—lots of bacon—cinnamon toast, orange juice, and coffee," Sage replied.

"I'll bring it to you in the library."

"Oh, and Alyce, could I have a steak for dinner tonight? With mushrooms and onions and that horseradish sauce you make, and a salad with your bleu-cheese dressing." The cook beamed at the request.

———————⊕———————

Lyle jumped to his feet when Sage came into the room. He hugged her and kissed her forehead, leading her to the chair he vacated. Before she sat, Sage stood beside Morgan and kissed her cheek.

"It's good to be home," Sage said and sat. She looked into Morgan's black eyes. "How long?"

"You've been asleep for almost two days. How are you feeling?"

"Weak and hungry, otherwise I'm okay," she absently rubbed her left arm, and looked questioningly at the old sorceress.

"I healed it; there won't even be a scar. How did that happened?"

Alyce took that moment to knock lightly and walked in with a tray filled with food. Sage ate in silence for a few minutes, relishing the smoky taste of the bacon and the acidic tang of the orange juice.

"Feel better now?" Morgan asked, not suppressing her grin.

"Much! Some kind of oatmeal for breakfast, usually no lunch, and soup or stew for dinner. I was always hungry. Oh, and I really dislike rabbit," Sage responded, sipping at her coffee and thoroughly enjoying the bitter brew.

"Sage, dear, how long were you there, and *where* were you?" Lyle blurted out before Morgan could ask.

"Since there were no newspapers or radio, I would guess the time around mid-summer of 1863, and I was close to the frontlines of the Civil War. In fact, I *was* at the frontline when I appeared, and that's when I was shot. It was only a graze, and it hurt like hell!" She paused to sip more of her coffee, relishing the strong flavor. "The doctor and hospital conditions were…dismal at best. Oh, and I was mistaken for a nurse that fortunately for me, never showed up. From the accents, I think it was somewhere in North Carolina, I can't be sure though. I do know I was on the Union side of the action." She smiled at Lyle, "and thanks for the soap!"

"How long were you there, Sage?" Morgan pressed.

"Almost two weeks," she answered, and then looked away, seeing the distant past.

"What did you do during all that time?" Lyle asked, bringing her back to the now.

"I taught them about hygiene and how to sterilize bandages and surgical instruments. The hospital was really horrible at first. It was a place to die, not get well. I helped change that."

"Was that your…mission?" Morgan asked.

"In part, I think. What I did got the attention of a doctor on the Confederate side, and he had me kidnapped."

"Kidnapped?"

"He wanted to know what I was doing that was saving lives," another sip of coffee calmed Sage enough to continue. "Even that wasn't why I was there. That doctor was ready to destroy a young man's life by unnecessarily amputating his arms, and I stopped him." She looked into Morgan's eyes before going on. "That young man was Humphrey Tuttle."

Morgan and Lyle both gasped.

"Wasn't it tempting to let Tuttle die?" Lyle huffed.

"Lyle, dear, this would have been Humphrey's father that Sage saved." Morgan took Sage's hand. "What do you see as the purpose to this?"

"It quickly occurred to me that if Tuttle senior was maimed or died, there would be no Tuttle junior. No Tuttle junior would mean Helen had no reason to be on the *Titanic*, and she might have stayed in England, and all of us wouldn't be right here, right now, in this house."

Morgan smiled as Lyle realized the implication.

"Was the kidnapping the trauma I see in your aura, Sage?" Morgan asked gently.

"No," she replied. "I was falling in love with a man that has now been dead for over one-hundred-fifty years."

CHAPTER SEVENTEEN

───────•❉•───────

"I n love?" Lyle clapped his hands. "Do tell! I want all the details."

"Lyle, give Sage a chance to recover before grilling her," Morgan admonished him.

"Oh, it's okay, Morgan. I think the sooner I talk about it, the sooner I can put it behind me, in the past where it belongs. The doctor at the hospital, Edward Colter, came across quite a jerk at first. Harsh, crude, with what seemed like deplorable skills; he also had a kind and generous heart that surfaced, along with a willingness to learn," Sage said. "And don't look at me that way, Lyle; I did *not* end up in his bed. Had I stayed much longer I may have though." She looked away wistfully. "I've been surrounded by death and sickness for weeks. I need some alone time. If you two don't mind, I'm going to the solarium for a while." She picked up her unfinished tray and left the room.

Morgan sighed in contemplation. "I need to think." She left the library for her rooms, leaving Lyle sitting there.

"Oh, well, I guess I'll go home," he said aloud though no one was near enough to hear him.

Hours later, Sage made her way through the dimly lit hallways and stopped in front of Morgan's chambers. She raised her fist to knock when the door swung open.

"Come in child, and tell me what's on your mind."

With tears in her eyes, she knelt beside Morgan's chair. "Can you make me forget him?"

"I could, but I think you need to remember this man. In time the pain will pass, and you will have fond thoughts of him. Give it time."

Sage bent her head in acceptance.

"What else is troubling you?" Morgan questioned.

"I thought these time travel ventures were to correct or change something in *your* past; something *you* did. Twice now that hasn't held true. I'm confused."

"These two trips seemed to have unfolded for you to ensure this timeline. And you've done remarkably well, Sage. The next time may be something completely different."

"I'm not sure I want a next time." Sage stood.

"And I'm not sure I can stop a next time from happening," Morgan confessed. "The power in the crystals, the star stones, is stronger than I've ever seen it and still growing, and it wants *you* to fix something, Sage. *You.*"

"I'm so tired, Morgan."

"I know. I think you need a vacation this time, to recuperate. Where would you like to go?"

"I'm glad you said where and not when!" Sage gave her a sad smile. "And to answer your question, I don't know, just away."

"Oh, Alyce, that was perfect," Sage sighed with content. Dinner had been a medium-rare, premium ribeye steak, fresh mushrooms sautéed with sweet onions, plus Alyce's special horseradish sauce, and green beans from the greenhouse gardens. She had first been served a salad of crunchy romaine, fresh peas, and buttermilk bleu cheese dressing. Her hunger was finally satisfied.

"More cabernet?" Jon asked Sage, while addressing Lyle and Morgan too.

"Thank you, Jon," Sage said pushing her glass closer to him. "I don't care if I see another glass of ale. I will admit it was safer to drink that than the water!" The other three watched as she smiled sadly.

"I think Sage has decided where she would like to go on vacation," Morgan announced.

"Yes, I have. Some place warm that also has air conditioning if it's too hot. And somewhere I can find quiet, yet also has an exciting night life, and has shopping, and beaches."

"Sounds delicious!" Lyle said with a grin. "Where can you find all that?"

"Key West," she replied, "And…"

"And what?" Morgan asked, already knowing what Sage would say.

"And I would like us all to go." She turned to Lyle and Jon. "Can you two take the time off?"

"The advantage of working freelance is we can do whatever we want," Lyle said. "We will have to do some shopping before we leave though."

"I was going to ask you to take me, Lyle. I trust your taste above my own." Sage smiled when Lyle blushed.

"How much time do we have?" Jon asked, looking at Morgan.

"I will need to make a few calls, but I would say within the week we could leave."

"Oh, this is going to be so much fun!" Jon grinned. "A whole week in the Keys."

"I was thinking of two weeks," Sage said. Morgan calmly nodded.

CHAPTER EIGHTEEN

---***---

The four friends left the plush first class lounge at the Manhattan Airport when the flight to Miami was announced. The TSA agent stopped Morgan.

"I'm sorry lady, you can't take that cane with you. A flight attendant will check it and give it back to you after you land," the chubby agent smirked.

"You won't deny an old lady her only means of walking, will you." Morgan stated, not asking, keeping her voice low and quiet.

He looked momentarily confused. "Oh, of course not. Have a pleasant flight. Next!" He looked past the other three as if they weren't there.

Once they were settled in their oversized plush seats in the first-class section of the jet, Jon started to giggle.

"You sure are handy to have when traveling!"

"He was being...overzealous in his job," she said. "Besides, this staff never leaves my side."

The short flight was pleasant, with a small meal and free drinks that Jon took full advantage of. As they were landing in Miami, Lyle whispered to Sage, "I think Jon is drunk." Morgan overheard, stood and tapped Jon on the head from her seat behind him. He was instantly sober.

Once they were off the large commercial jet, the pilot for their private craft met them immediately.

"If you will let me have your luggage claims, I will have your baggage transferred over. Please follow me, I will escort you to the boarding dock," the polite young man said, professionally taking over.

That flight was even shorter but just as smooth and soon they were landing at a private airport outside of Key West.

———◆———

Sage stepped out onto the stairway that had quickly appeared after their craft came to a halt, and took a deep breath. A soft warm breeze cooled the sweat that was already forming on her forehead.

"There is nothing like the salty smell of Caribbean heat and humidity," she said with a satisfied smile.

"We're not in the Caribbean, Sage," Jon quickly reminded her.

"Close enough for me!" she replied. She quickly descended the metal steps, and then waited patiently for the other three to join her. When all four were on the small and well maintained tarmac, a limo pulled up beside them and started loading their luggage.

Morgan handed the driver a brochure of the place they were renting. He nodded and returned it to her.

"Is he sure where he's going?" Lyle questioned nervously, a few minutes later. "All these back streets…"

The driver smiled into the mirror and continued on his way, finally stopping in front of a large house, one of the many *painted ladies* on the island. . He opened the door for Morgan and said, "I will wait here while you collect the key code and then take you to the unit."

All four emerged from the air-conditioned car and with Morgan in the lead, went into what turned out to be an office that oversaw a number of rental units.

"Good afternoon," a dark tanned portly man of undeterminable age greeted them. "I'm Alfred Picard. You must be the Alsteen party. Do come in, it's warm out there today. I have your guide packets ready for you, one for each. Your key code is printed at the top of the first page."

"What is the code for?" Sage asked.

"It's to the lock box that holds the keys to the house. The code is changed after every tenant has departed: much easier than constantly changing the locks," he laughed heartedly. "The lock box is mounted inside the mailbox so it's less obvious. Inside there are six keys; please take all six out and leave the extras on the kitchen table; the housekeeper will return them to me after you leave and I will change the code. Do you have any questions?"

"The housekeeper is the only one with access while we're here?" Morgan asked.

"She only has access when you notify me you need her services, that's when I give her a key and she returns it to me when she's done. She never has the code until after you leave," he explained.

"Sounds like a secure system," Jon commented.

"Enjoy your stay," he smiled broadly.

---------◆---------

After Sage retrieved the keys and opened the door, the limo driver carried Morgan's luggage into the house, while the other three carried their own.

Morgan tipped him generously, as usual.

"Thank you, ma'am," he said, pocketing the bill without even glancing at it. "If there is any place you would like to go on the island that is not within walking distance, please give me a call," he handed her a card that simply read "Geoffrey" and a cellphone number.

"Nice place," Lyle said after the driver departed. As a group, they roamed throughout, scrutinizing the various rooms. They found two bedrooms on the upper level with curtained French doors leading to small balconies, plus a shared full bath. Two more large bedrooms on the main floor with private baths, along with the kitchen, a dining area, and an expansive living room with a flat screen TV and an impressive sound system.

"I'm taking a bedroom on the main floor," Morgan stated. "Sage, if you would take the one beside me, I would appreciate it. You two can have whichever rooms you want on the second floor. And once everyone settles in, I say we find a place for lunch; I'm famished."

Lyle put Morgan's case on the bed for her. "Are you feeling okay?" he asked her, concerned, after seeing her hands shake.

"I'm fine, just a little tired from the trip. I can put things away; why don't you help Jon pick a room."

When he was up the stairs, Morgan tapped on Sage's door and let herself in. "I'd like you to wear this at all times while we're here." She removed the star stone crystal from her wrist, the enchanted serpent yawned and seemed to smile to be free, even if only for a short time.

"Sure, but why?" Sage asked while Morgan draped it around her neck. "Don't you need it?"

"First of all, it will keep you safe; and you forget, there are two that can be worn and the third one is always inside the staff. I'm wearing mine now. Unpack what you need to and get comfortable. I'm hungry!" Morgan didn't explain that even maintaining her youthful appearance taxed her metabolism and burned up vast amounts of calories.

Dressed casually, Sage in a knee length split skirt and tank top, the two men in shorts and t-shirts, and Morgan in cool linen slacks with a loose blouse, the four found a port-side diner and took seats out on the viewing deck.

"What a wonderful idea this was," Morgan said, peeling a well-chilled shrimp and devouring it in two bites.

"Here's to Sage, for inviting us along," Lyle picked up his glass of chardonnay in toast. Jon meanwhile slurped another raw oyster and gave his partner a wink.

"According to this map, Duval Street is only two streets over," Sage explained after eating several shrimp dipped in the spicy sauce. "I'd like to do some shopping."

"What are you looking for?" Morgan asked.

"I don't know, but I'll know it when I see it." Sage smiled at her three friends. "There was a time when I would shop for gifts for my best friends while I was on vacation. But you are all here, which I think is the best gift of all." Morgan felt a pleasant flush at Sage's words.

The four meandered toward Duval Street, stopping to look in windows or watch jugglers perform. Sage went into a small shop that was tightly tucked in between two other shops sporting cheap t-shirts.

The quiet enveloped her and she knew her smile was wistful as she turned to take in the rows of brightly colored bottles, half-glasses filled with incense sticks and a variety of knick-knacks on almost every surface.

"Can I help you find something, miss?" a wizened old woman suddenly appeared from the depths of the store.

"Maybe. What's in the bottles?"

"Ah, oils and fragrances I use to customize perfume," she explained.

"How is it you can customize a perfume? Isn't a scent a personal thing?" Sage questioned.

"Indeed, it is. The way scented oil reacts on the skin of the wearer changes, and becomes something different to whoever smells it. Take this for example," the merchant picked up a small cobalt-blue bottle and removed the stopper, offering it to Sage for a sniff. "What does it smell like to you?"

"Burning leaves," Sage wrinkled her nose in distaste.

The merchant put a dot on her own hand, rubbed it, and offered it again to Sage. "Now that it has interacted with my own chemistry, what do you smell?"

"Lily of the Valley flowers! That's remarkable. How would you customize a scent for…me?"

"Give me your hand," the old lady requested and briefly closed her gray eyes while holding Sage's hand, then she put a dot of a different oil on Sage's wrist, and a dab of a second bottle. "What do you smell?"

Sage cautiously lifted her hand and smelled. "Soft, musky, hibiscus."

"And on me it would be different."

"How do you know which oils to use?" Sage questioned.

"It's a gift I have."

"Can you make me a small bottle of that?" Sage was delighted with the scent. As the old woman worked behind the counter, Sage continued to wander the store until she spotted a table with various brass figurines and selected one.

"Wear this carefully, young lady, it will make you irresistible to men," the old lady smiled devilishly.

Sage ran her deep-blue debit card through the reader device and left with her purchases. Stepping out of the small shop, she spotted the trio sitting at a wicker bistro table sipping drinks.

"And what did you find, Sage?" Morgan asked.

She produced a highly polished six-inch brass crab that hid an ashtray in its body, and the small golden bottle. "This is a perfume that is supposed to make me irresistible." She laughed and handed Morgan the tiny bottle.

Morgan sniffed and said, "I don't smell anything at all." Then Sage offered her wrist, and Morgan sniffed again. "Hmm, hibiscus. Very interesting."

Jon picked up Sage's hand and smelled her wrist and gave her a smile. Lyle did so also, again, smiling. "I've always found you irresistible," he said and kissed the back of her hand.

CHAPTER NINETEEN

------◆------

"**H**ave you rested enough, Morgan?" Lyle asked. "I understand the Atocha Museum is just around the corner. I've always wanted to see a real bar of gold!" His enthusiasm was high and made it impossible for Morgan to resist.

The ship Atocha sank off the coast of the Florida Keys during a storm in 1622 and rested there until 1985, when Mel Fisher discovered it after years of searching. The museum on the historic sunken treasure find was nearly empty of curious tourists, and the foursome wandered casually from locked cases, to framed pictures, and finally to a Plexiglas display where Lyle slipped his hand into the provided slot, and picked up a heavy bar of gold. The case was designed that no matter how the bar was turned it could not be removed from its transparent safe. He smiled in satisfaction and set the bar down again.

"Don't you want a piece of sunken treasure jewelry, Sage?" Lyle asked, having noticed Sage's penchant for finely crafted items.

"I will admit it's tempting, and this piece is lovely, but I have on the best piece of jewelry ever," she said, fingering the sleeping serpent around her neck, who purred gently into her skin.

115

"Let's take the Conch Train Tour," Morgan announced. "It will give us an idea of what to see tomorrow and give me a chance to sit."

After the tour, they stopped at the Butterfly Conservatory and then finished their afternoon with a visit to the Margaritaville bar. Non-stop Buffet songs greeted them and they claimed the only empty table.

"Whew, I must say this has been a very full day," Sage said, sipping her frosty drink. "Thank you all for joining me. I know this was very touristy today, I think tomorrow I'm going to sit on a beach somewhere."

⁕

"Lyle, the next time you and Jon are out and about, I'd like you to stop back at the Atocha museum and buy that emerald ring Sage was admiring," Morgan said, handing him a deep-blue credit card. "Her birthday is coming up soon, and I want to surprise her."

⁕

The days slipped past. Days filled with walking and laughter, with casual dining, and sightseeing. They visited Hemingway's house and all his cats, and had lunch at Sloppy Joe's. Sage finally began to relax, and her recent trip into the past was fading.

"If I weren't hungry, I would suggest staying in today," Sage dropped into a kitchen chair across from Lyle and Jon. A pure-white polydactyl cat jumped into her lap. "Where did this charmer come from?" she stroked his soft fur and gently examined his six-toed paws.

"I think he followed you home from the Hemingway House. I heard it's a law here that if one of Hemingway's cats follow you home, you have to keep it," Jon teased her. "And while we were sightseeing yesterday and you were at the beach, Morgan went grocery shopping. The fridge is full, so take your pick. I think the only things off limits are the steaks marinating," Jon dug his hand into a bag of sugary donuts.

"I hope she got cat food." Sage made a bacon and egg sandwich for breakfast and then sat alone in the fenced in yard to enjoy it, sharing pieces with the cat she named Paws.

"Something bothering you, dear?" Morgan quietly appeared in the yard.

"Not a thing, although…" Sage hesitated, "yesterday I was looking at the piers and saw one of the smaller cruise ships. They have two-day cruises that will go to Havana, and then over to Nassau, and then back here. The weather forecast is clear." Sage had been drawn to the cruise ship for some reason she couldn't explain.

"Havana? Well, that might be interesting now that the US and Cuba have good relationships again. When would you like to go? Tomorrow?"

"I know you have steaks planned for tonight, so tomorrow I'd like to do the Mallory Square sunset and have dinner there if that's alright. We can do the cruise after that."

"Whatever you want, Sage." Morgan knew she was pampering the girl, even to the point of buttering her up…for the next time travel, which may prove more delicate, and more dangerous, than the previous excursions.

"I think that was the best conch chowder I've ever had," Morgan stated, pushing her bowl away. They had scored a prime viewing table for dinner and the coming sunset. Although the restaurant was five-star dining, dress was still casual. The men wore shorts and new short sleeved flowered shirts and sandals; Sage had on a dark caramel halter sundress that barely touched her knees and showed off her deepening tan; Morgan wore her usual long dark split skirt and a new flowered blouse—her concession to shopping, which she detested doing.

"I agree, it was awesome. And this sampler tray was a great idea, Sage." Lyle shelled another chilled shrimp, dipped it in the garlic butter sauce, and chewed it thoughtfully.

"There are so many good things on the menu it was hard to decide what to order. The conch fritters are pretty good too, and I know Jon likes the raw oysters, so the sampler made it the perfect selection. Have you tried the lobster pieces?" Sage asked. Although she was tasting from the variety plate, she had settled on a lobster salad as her main dish.

"A salad? Sweetie, you can't be dieting; you're already so thin," Jon was quick to point out with a tsk in his voice.

"Don't forget that tomorrow we leave on a two-day cruise, where the food is heralded as being some of the best and there's always plenty of it," Sage reminded them, "and I plan on trying a lot of it."

Their plates had been cleared away and a second bottle of wine was opened. Sunset was getting close. From their vantage point on the raised dining deck, it was clear that no one could block the view that was coming.

"After the sun sets, I'd like to mingle. I read there are fire jugglers, and singers, and various street performers that we can't see from here. Please watch your wallets and purses. Events like this always bring out riff-raff and pickpockets," Morgan cautioned.

"Since no one would dare accost *you*, Morgan, I say you get to be the keeper of our wallets," Jon suggested, handing her his billfold, as did Lyle. "What about you, Sage?"

"This over the shoulder purse has a security clip on it. Besides, all anyone would find is my lip gloss, a comb, hanky, and a few dollars." A roar went up in the crowd below them, and someone started a countdown. "Look! There goes the sun. Isn't it beautiful the way the colors shimmer on the water? The sun looks like it is actually sizzling!"

They each took a plastic cup filled with the remainder of the wine and wandered down to the crowded pier.

"I've been meaning to ask you something, if it's not too personal," Sage said to Morgan.

"What is it, child?"

"You seem to enjoy wine as much as the rest of us, although it never seems to affect you. How is that?"

Morgan laughed. "I love the taste of wine—all wines: reds, whites, blends, champagnes. I refuse to lose control though, and I adjust my metabolism when I drink. Did you notice how I sobered Jon on the plane? It's an easy trick. If you want to continue drinking without the effects, let me know."

"Lovely lady, come dance with me!" A tall, dark, young man tugged on Sage's arm, sloshing her drink. Jon quickly relieved her of the cup, with a devilish grin.

She danced two lively songs with the attractive man, and the steel drum band slowed the tempo down. He pulled her close to him.

"You smell like flowers in the morning before the heat of the day," he leaned even closer, inhaling her new perfume. "That is a most intriguing necklace you have on. Is that real gold?"

"Gold? It's an enchanted serpent," she teased and felt the serpent tense. Sometimes the best lie is the truth made to sound like a lie.

"Enchanted? How delightful," he said, running his finger along her collarbone in an obvious seductive distraction and then along the chain, looking for the clasp. The serpent growled, nipped the young man's finger, and blinked its red eyes, instantly resuming its passive state. The man went wide-eyed and backed up, rubbing his finger.

"Oh, it doesn't like you," Sage said with a pout and turned away to rejoin her friends, giggling.

"Why did that man run off like he did?" Morgan asked.

Sage leaned in close. "The serpent growled at him for touching him."

Morgan looked around for the man who was now nowhere in sight and laughed heartedly. She then looked closely at the serpent and noticed a dot of blood on a golden fang. "Did the serpent bite him?"

"I don't know, why?"

"The bite of a dragon is always fatal," Morgan said thoughtfully. "I told you it would protect you and it has. They have irrefutable sense of who is good and who is evil. Always trust it."

"Dragon? I thought it was a serpent," Sage said.

"A dragon, serpent, or snake are all reptiles, and in magic they are the same only in different forms. Some are deadlier than others, but they are all faithful to their master. Come, Jon and Lyle are getting their fortunes read, and I want to hear."

"…And you have an impressive flair for colors. You are hiding a great secret though," the psychic said, holding Lyle's hand.

"Oh, no great secret, I came out of the closet quite some time ago," Lyle refuted, smiling.

"That's not the secret you hold close to you," she touched Jon's hand with her other. "You share this secret. You both love the same woman."

Jon laughed, "secret is out, Lyle, and here she comes. Morgan, this woman is a delight! It will be most interesting what she has to say about *you*." His eyes twinkled with mirth.

"I think Sage should go next, I'm such a boring person," Morgan grinned.

Lyle stood and gave his seat to Sage. "Where is that young man you were dancing with? I was hoping you would get lucky tonight," he teased.

"I would say he didn't like my necklace, except my necklace didn't like *him*," Sage responded with a knowing grin. She set her hand on the table for the psychic, who placed it between hers and closed her eyes.

"You've had many losses this past year and your heart is heavy with grief. Both your parents? Plus, friends and lovers—no, not lovers—would be lovers. Do not fret, you will be reunited."

"Fat chance," Lyle mumbled to Jon, and Jon snickered.

Sage started to pull her hand away, but the woman held fast. "You have much traveling ahead of you. I see two more trips, and it will be painful. Trust in yourself, and you will be fine." She let go of Sage's hand and looked at Morgan, holding out her hand.

"You really don't want to do this," Morgan said softly.

"You're right, I don't, however you need me to," was the response and the woman clasped both of Morgan's hands before she could move away...

...and instantly swayed in agony. "You have such pain inside of you ever since...forever. *She* will resolve it for you, but don't push it, just...go with the flow."

She looked into Morgan's black eyes. "Such power, such ancient power you keep in check; it's consuming you; it hurts so much. Find a way to let it out." The old woman let go of Morgan's hand and wept.

Sage took a large bill from her small purse and put it in the woman's tip jar. Morgan placed her hand on the weeping woman's shoulder and whispered so only she could hear, "Thank you. Be at peace."

The four walked away in silence while the woman forgot they had been there.

The handsome dark man started to feel woozy within minutes after running from the odd encounter. His hand throbbed and was swelling. Realizing something was seriously wrong, he headed for the nearest medical clinic.

"There isn't anything I can tell you, officer," the clinic nurse said. "I came out to the waiting room to take him to see the doctor, and that's how I found him: slumped in the chair, unresponsive."

"Did you examine him, doctor?" the officer addressed the resident physician.

"Briefly, and I found two small puncture marks on the anterior side of the right index finger that appear to be from a small snake," the doctor replied.

"Do you have any idea what kind of a snake?"

"You know we are capable of certain procedures because of our isolation, so I ran a quick blood test for toxins to determine if there was something here we need to be aware of." The doctor frowned.

"What did you find?" the officer asked.

"This young man was bitten alright, and it would appear to be by an asp or from the asp family," the doctor said, "although that seems unlikely. Asps are not indigenous to the area. I'm sending a sample to the mainland for a further analysis."

Officer Jenkins ran an ID on the victim, and found a rap sheet full of priors, all dealing with theft. He added his notes from the evening and closed the case. This petty thief wouldn't be a problem anymore.

CHAPTER TWENTY

———————◆❀◆———————

"**N**ow, we'll only be gone two nights so don't over pack," Morgan warned. "If you forget something we can always get it on the ship or in one of the ports. One thing to remember, dining on board is always dressy, and don't leave anything valuable behind; housekeeping will come in while we're gone."

Geoffrey put the four weekend bags in the back of the limo and drove them to the wide wooden pier where the *Midnight Princess* was moored.

"I thought you said this was a *small* ship," Jon leaned back looking up the side.

"This *is* small compared to some of the other cruise liners," Sage replied. "You should have seen how big the *Titanic* was." She turned to Morgan. "I hope this is one of the trips the psychic mentioned, and don't think for a second I forgot about that." Morgan feigned ignorance. Sage turned her attention back to Jon. "Most cruise ships have occupancy of twenty-five hundred guests, and a crew of over a thousand. The *Midnight Princess* hosts half of that. She's a new ship and faster than most. The brochure says by leaving in the morning for nearby Havana we will arrive in plenty of time for a full afternoon on the island. Then in the evening and overnight, we cruise to Nassau for another full day and spend a second night returning to Key West."

"Since this is *your* vacation, Sage, what do you want to do at our ports of call?" Lyle asked, as they continued up the wide gangway where the concierge waited for all guests to hand them over to a porter.

"Since for most of my life, Cuba was off limits for travel, I'd like to wander a bit. I hear the local food is wonderful, and the cathedrals are beautiful, and, of course, the weather and the area is…breath taking. I think I'd like to see a cigar factory, too," Sage answered, getting more enthused by the minute. "I'm not sure about Nassau. I say we…go with the flow." She gave Morgan a sheepish grin.

Finally, a porter greeted them and loaded their luggage on a cart. He looked at their room assignments and smiled broadly. They followed the young man whose name tag read "Peter—Germany", to the elevator and up to the eighth deck.

Peter opened the doors to three suites and waited for them to say where the luggage went.

"This is mine, and I will take the center suite. You three can fight over the other two, except they are all the same." Morgan entered the middle room with Peter following, carrying her bag. He set the suitcase on a fold out luggage table and stepped over to the outer door and pulled back the drapes to expose the balcony.

Morgan handed him a hundred-dollar bill. "All charges *and tips* come to me. Understood?"

"Yes, ma'am!" he tipped his head in a slight bow, and stepped back into the hall, where the other three cases had disappeared.

Sage quickly unpacked her small suitcase and hung her two dresses in the closet so the wrinkles could fall out. Her toiletries went in the small and efficient bathroom; her jewelry went into the room safe and all else stayed in the bag. She wandered around the suite, smelling the fresh flowers and smiling. When she opened the drapes and saw the balcony, she giggled, and stepped out to find Morgan out on hers as well. They were soon joined by Lyle and Jon.

"Isn't this rather extravagant, Morgan?" Lyle pointed out.

"Not really, dear; when I called about three rooms, they offered me these balcony suites at a discount. It seems they are under-booked right now with it off season," she explained. "And did you notice the chilled bottle of champagne on the counter next to the refrigerator? I suggest we open them one at a time." Morgan looked at her three companions and smiled broadly. It was good to have...friends.

They were finishing the second bottle when the ships horn blasted, signaling they were about to set sail. The four had moved to Morgan's balcony, popped the cork on the final bottle and toasted to the journey, waving farewell to the onlookers congregating on the docks below them as the ship left Key West for the clear waters of the Caribbean.

"Now that we have been typical cruise tourists, I say we find the breakfast buffet and have something to eat," Sage suggested. "The directions say all food handling is aft. Is that front or back?"

"It's the back, dear, as opposed to forward which is...forward," Morgan said with a snicker, linking arms with Sage and heading back to the elevators and deck three.

"I'm almost sorry we drank all three bottles of bubbly," Lyle said. "Now we'll have to track someone down to order more."

"Come on, we'll have mimosas with our eggs," Jon offered.

"Those two are really enjoying themselves," Sage whispered to Morgan.

"Yes, they are. Aren't you?" Morgan seemed worried.

"I'm having a grand time, Morgan. Don't worry about me. I have a feeling this is going to be a memorable trip."

The buffet was everything they expected and then some. Sage took raspberry crepes drizzled with thick rich cream, sausage links, and bacon. She looked around for the coffee and juice, and then noticed a carafe of the hot brew on each table, as well as a pitcher of chilled orange juice, much like it was on the *Titanic*. A cloud passed across her mind and left as quickly.

Peter appeared at Morgan's side and offered to show them to their assigned table. Morgan took the opportunity to whisper something to him, which he nodded to.

After they had feasted, Lyle and Jon took off for the casino, which had opened once they hit international water, and Sage and Morgan found lounge chairs to enjoy the sun and ocean breezes.

"You seem pensive, Sage," Morgan knew the girl was nervous about the next trip.

"Pensive; interesting word, meaning quietly sad or thoughtful. I guess you could say that's how I feel about another time visit," Sage bit her lower lip in thought. "Do you have any idea when or where this might be?"

"Not yet, though I'm fairly certain this time will, indeed, involve me, or perhaps I should say, a past me."

As they passed one of the ballrooms on their way back from breakfast, Sage heard music and peeked inside. An older man was giving ballroom lessons to a small group. He had salt and pepper hair, cut longish and looked to be in very good physical shape, obviously from the regular dancing. Sage watched in interest for a minute, noting he was also very attractive, then continued on to catch up with the group.

Elem Houser stopped in midsentence and looked at the doorway. No one was there; he was sure he had felt a familiar presence, but only saw a shadow of someone walking past. Shaking it off, he resumed teaching this group how to do the basic box step that was essential to not only the waltz and the fox trot, but many other dances as well.

CHAPTER TWENTY ONE

------ ◈ ------

A lthough lunch was available to those who elected to stay on board, most opted to go ashore and see the sights of Havana as well as partake of some local food.

"The Partagás, the most famous cigar factory in Cuba, is a gorgeous landmark with distinctive architecture that was built in 1845," Jon read the brochure that was encased in plexiglass outside the old and weathered building. Morgan paid the tour fee for them, and they entered, stepping back in time.

"The cigars here are still hand made," the guide said with a heavy accent, "without the use of mechanical rollers," he boasted. "Please watch your step, ladies, the marble floors are worn very smooth and might be slippery." The rich scent of fresh tobacco leaves greeted them.

Jon and Lyle made a purchase on their way out, and the group reassembled on the corner of the crumbling street.

They wandered the main streets, visiting new boutiques housed in very old buildings. They stopped to watch a street performer play a lively tune on a twelve-string guitar, and Jon left a sizeable tip.

They found an open-air taxi and took a short tour of the island sights. Lush vegetation reached out along the narrow road as the guide pointed out various attractions and monuments.

Closer to the ships dock, Morgan suggested they sit for a while at a nearby bistro and have a light lunch.

"This Cuban sandwich looks wonderful, and awfully big," Morgan said. "It has roast pork, ham, Swiss cheese, dill pickles, and spicy yellow mustard on their famous and unique Cuban bread. Who wants to split one with me?"

"I will," Sage was quick to respond.

Jon and Lyle decided to do the same, and they all ordered a mojito, a tangy rum drink, to go with it.

Back on board the cruise liner, everyone opted for a nap before dinner.

CHAPTER TWENTY TWO

———————◆❋◆———————

S age woke from her nap at six o'clock. Knowing dinner started at seven, she took a quick shower, refreshed her makeup and selected a dress.

"Oh, that blue silk does look lovely on you!" Lyle complimented. "It compliments your eyes and the stone. I'm so delighted it survived its trip from the *Titanic*!"

"And I'm sure these heels look better than those boots I had on," she laughed, then sobered. "I left those boots in 1863, Lyle. I loved the way they fit."

"I will find you another pair, my dear, don't fret."

"And another green sweater?"

"Yes, and another green sweater."

The four took the elevator to the second deck where the main dining hall was located in the aft section. Once again, Peter spotted them coming in and greeted them all by first name.

"Did you have a pleasant afternoon in port?" he asked, guiding them to their assigned table.

"It was delightful, Peter, and thank you for replenishing our champagne," Jon said with a twinkle in his eyes. Morgan smiled.

"The dinner buffet will open shortly. May I interest you in a bottle of wine?" Peter said.

———•◦❋◦•———

"Oh my, they certainly have lived up to their reputation for exceptional food," Morgan sighed with content. The other two couples that joined them at the table for eight, agreed. When the dessert cart started to make the rounds, everyone passed, though opted for coffee or tea.

Shortly the band arrived, relieving the young man who was quietly playing a guitar as soft dinner music. They continued to play quietly to not interfere with the table conversation, though they did pick up the pace.

Sage looked around the large room, gently swaying with the music. She spotted him across the dance floor, talking with the occupants of a larger table. She stood and walked in that direction, a vision of beauty, deep blue silk flowing around her legs, caressing her shapely calves.

"Excuse me," she said. "Would you dance with me?"

Elem gasped at the vision in front of him: the deep blue silk plunged at the neckline meeting ribbons of the same color, long sleeves hung loose enough to not restrain her arms, and the hemline skimmed above the ankle straps of her heeled shoes. "I don't believe I saw you in one of my classes. I definitely would have remembered." The dark blue crystal stone at her throat beckoned to him.

"I don't need classes," she said smiling. "I just need someone to dance with that I know won't step on my toes." That gained her a smile from him.

Elem led her to the dance floor in front of the band, and said something to them. They struck up a waltz. He started gently.

"Ah, I see you don't need lessons," Elem smiled down at her, guiding her efficiently. "Think you can keep up?"

"If you can lead, I can follow," Sage replied.

"Then let's give them a show," he picked up the challenge. For a moment they locked eyes, both remembering the familiar exchange.

The waltz, with multiple direction shifts and spins, morphed into a fox trot, and then into a lively, sexy tango. Sage laughed as the tango ended with her in a deep dip.

"That was delightful!" Elem said, as the crowd applauded their performance. Then he got serious. "I know you. I don't know from where or when, but I do know you, Miss...."

"Aster, Sage Aster," she studied his face, the graying hair, the deep smile lines; nothing was familiar, except his eyes, the soft welcoming brown eyes she had looked into before.

He shook his head in frustration. "It's all there, on the edge of my memory, like a shadow I can't quite focus on. Perhaps in time it will come to me. Thank you for the dances, Miss Sage Aster," He bowed slightly and kissed her hand. "I'm on the clock. I need to dance with some of my students. I hope to see you later."

Sage sat down at her table and the other seven gave her another round of quiet, yet enthusiastic, applause.

"That was beautiful, Sage. I didn't know you could dance like that!" Lyle was the first to comment on her expertise.

"I started taking ballroom dancing lessons when I was twelve. And that was after years of solo box-step practicing with a mat on the floor," Sage confessed. "It's called muscle memory: you repeat something so many times, it becomes natural." She glanced in Elem's direction and found him staring at her. She smiled in return.

"So, tomorrow we should wake up in Nassau. What are we going to do there?" Jon quickly changed the subject.

"Shop!" Sage announced. "I need a new dress for dinner tomorrow night."

CHAPTER TWENTY THREE

------------◦✸◦------------

T he foursome became six when one of the couples from the night before joined them on the docks. As before, they wandered the streets, this time marveling at the canopy of colorful bougainvillea flowers, pruned into a long arch. Unlike Havana, Nassau was a hive of activity, with street merchants selling everything from sponges harvested from the ocean floor, to painted fish scales crafted into earrings. Every street was swept clean and every corner had a liquor store, selling locally made rums and the favorite drink of the island, the sweet Nassau Royale.

Anytime they found a clothing boutique, Sage ducked in to check the quality of the merchandise. What she wanted wasn't going to be cheap nor would it be easy to find.

"Lyle!" she called out from one of the doorways. He joined her at a rack of flowing silk dresses in a variety of colors and lengths.

"What do you think of this one? It's a shade of red you can wear." He had pulled out a sleeveless red dress in a soft figure molding stretch Lycra material, with a flared skirt and fitted waistline.

"Oh, my, that is beautiful. Wait right here," she took the dress from his hands and disappeared into a tiny fitting room. When she emerged moments later, Lyle grinned. Before him stood Sage, the red dress caressed her skin like it was made for her; the neckline was a low scoop, the back was a few crisscrossing thin strips, and the hem hit just above her knees. She turned in a circle and stopped, the skirt kept moving and swished around her.

"You are beautiful, my dear," he kissed her cheek. "Will you need jewelry to go with that?"

"No," she smiled slyly, "I brought something from home." Lyle's eyes went wide in understanding.

"It will look stunning. Spin again for me." He requested and she did so with a grin. "What you do need is some red undies!"

Sage paid for the items with her dark-blue debit card, plastic being the currency of choice at most of the tourist stops. She felt giddy with her find, and clutched the shopping bag tightly for the rest of the island stay.

"I say we have lunch at Black Beard's Tavern," Jon suggested. Morgan mumbled something about what a disagreeable man Edward Teach had been.

Sage leaned close to her and asked, "Did you really know him?"

"Yes, and he also smelled most foul!" she whispered back.

Cool air conditioning met them as they entered the busy restaurant. The hostess met them at the door. "The wait is a half hour. Name?"

"What about that table for six out on the deck?" Morgan pushed.

The hostess looked confused and checked her seating. "Hmm, I didn't see them leave. I'll have someone clear the table for you immediately."

"How lucky for us," their other companion said.

"Yes, we always seem to have the best luck when Morgan is with us," Sage chuckled. Nothing could ruin her good mood.

They ordered two large sampler platters and rum drinks, not wanting to quell their appetites to the point of spoiling their dinner on board the cruise ship.

———•❋•———

The six continued to causally wander the streets after their light lunch. Eventually the other couple decided to explore on their own and left the four looking at fishing schedules by the pier.

"I don't know, Jon. I'm concerned about being out on a boat when ours is ready to leave!" Lyle protested. "Besides, we can go fishing when we get back to Key West, right Morgan?"

"Absolutely you can. Remember though we only have a few more days in the Keys before our flight back to New York," she reminded them. "We'll arrange a fishing tour first thing when we get back, Jon. For now, I have to agree with Lyle's concern."

"I'd like to do some snorkeling," Sage said. "It was recommended when we left the ship that we take or wear a bathing suit. Did anyone else do that besides me?"

"I did not," Morgan emphatically stated, "I dislike swimming. If you two didn't bring swim trunks, there's a shop over there where you can buy one and rent the necessary equipment. And don't forget a towel."

An hour of off-shore snorkeling satisfied Sage's need to be in the warm Caribbean water looking at colorful fish, and the group was ready to head back to the ship.

"I'm going to take a short rest," Morgan stated when they arrived at the doors to their respective suites.

"I think I'll go up to the pool and swim a bit more, maybe work on my tan," Sage grinned.

"And we're going back to the casino," Lyle said.

Sage let herself into her room and hung the new dress in the tiny closet. She brushed her hand along the soft material. The material literally shed all wrinkles, stretched to enhance all curves and was machine washable. An ideal material, and best of all, it made Sage feel beautiful.

———————●———————

"Morgan?" Sage tapped lightly on their adjoining door.

"Come in, child. What…oh my, you look incredible! That must be the new dress you and Lyle were so excited about," Morgan's eyes shone with appreciation.

"Yes, and I think the ruby necklace would be perfect with this. Can you take the star stone off me and keep it for the evening?"

"Of course, my dear. You might need one of the boys to help you with the rubies though, my fingers are feeling stiff tonight." Morgan ran a finger down the serpent's head; it yawned and let go of its tail. Morgan wrapped it around her arm and the serpent went still again.

"Why don't you wear both around your neck?" Sage questioned.

Morgan looked down at the golden snake. "They can't come in contact with each other. Yes, they are enchanted, but they are also a mated pair. If they touch, the enchantment is broken."

Sage mulled this over. She had more questions, however she knew when Morgan ended a discussion.

Hours later the tight group made their way to the aft main dining room and was once again met and seated by Peter.

"Although there are several poultry dishes on the buffet tonight, I highly recommend the beef tenderloin tips. May I bring you some red wine?" he smiled at his group. All the porters had only two or three groups to handle, which was how they maintained a very personal touch. Peter liked his job as much as he genuinely liked the people he served. This group of friends was special. He could see it in the way they treated each other and deferred to the one named Morgan. Although she appeared to be in the same age bracket, her energy told him she was the elder of four. No matter, he thought, they were devoted to each other and that made them special to him.

"Red wine would be appreciated, Peter. Thank you," Morgan said. "Will you be seeing us off in the morning?" She wanted to be sure the healthy tip she was planning would end up in his hands alone.

"Of course, Morgan, I wouldn't miss the opportunity to say good bye and wish you well. I'll be right back with your wine."

Jon took the private moment to lean closer to Sage. "You look absolutely stunning tonight. You simply glow! If I didn't love Lyle, I would be in love with you!"

Once again, after the dishes were cleared away, the dessert cart arrived. Sage decided to splurge with a piece of cheesecake. As she ate, the woman across the table stared at her.

"That is a most intriguing necklace you have on Miss Aster. Those aren't real rubies, are they?" The woman finally asked.

"Christie's seem to think so," Sage said casually. "Thirty-two perfectly cut rubies of various sizes, plus forty smaller diamonds, set into gold *and* an antique; value estimated at 2.6 million dollars. That's what you wanted to know, isn't it?" Sage raised her eyebrow at the nosey woman.

"I was curious, yes," the woman stammered, embarrassed.

"It's not the Hope Diamond, but I'm rather fond of it," Sage added with a smile. She looked around the room and saw him. Elem Houser, handsome in his pristine white tuxedo, was headed in her direction.

"Miss Aster, you look lovely tonight," he said with a slight bow. "Would you do me the honor of this next dance?" Sage slid her hand into his without saying a word.

He immediately spun her into a turn that ended in his arms, and they began to dance.

"You look absolutely ravishing, Sage," his eyes lingered on the necklace. "I've seen that necklace before. Like I know you, I know those gems, and again like you, I don't know from where, but they mean something to me I can't remember." Sadness settled in his eyes, and then was gone. "That's for another time. Right now, I have the most beautiful woman on the ship in my arms and that's all that matters." He smiled widely, showing perfect white teeth, and spun her across the floor. Her soft red dress swirled around her legs, showing trim calves and thighs before settling again. His hand caressed her nearly bare back like a lover and his eyes saw only her.

Twenty minutes of music ended with another hearty round of applause.

"I can't let you go again, Sage, not until we talk," Elem pleaded.

"Morgan, I have some questions," Sage said while the two walked back to their rooms later.

"What has you so troubled, Sage?" the old sorceress asked once they were alone.

"Is reincarnation real?"

"Most definitely, why do you ask?"

"Because I think that dance instructor Elem Houser, is Ethan Woodhaven, Helen's brother. We dance like we did the night the *Titanic* sank, and we even spoke the same words and he says he knows me but can't remember," Sage babbled. "And his eyes are the same as Edward Colter. Could Edward have incarnated as Ethan, and then Ethan as Elem?"

Morgan paused to gather her thoughts. "It's possible. What do you want to do about it?"

"That gypsy psychic said we would be reunited."

"Are you saying you want to pursue a relationship with him? Sage, this Elem is old enough to be your grandfather."

"I don't see him as old, Morgan," Sage sobbed, "and I don't know what I want, all I know is that I'm lonely and I miss Edward. And Ethan and Elem both made me feel *alive* when dancing. Unless you dance it's hard to describe the emotions that come with moving as one. It feels as if we *are* one and meant to be together."

"I see." Morgan studied Sage's face as different emotions shifted through her eyes.

"Can you help him remember?"

"No! I won't do that. If, and it's a big *if,* he is the reincarnation of these two men you cared so deeply for, he has to remember on his own." Morgan saw the deep sorrow in Sage's eyes and it pained her. "Go back to your room and get some rest, my dear. We'll talk more in the morning." She helped Sage remove the ruby necklace and replaced it with the star stone from her wrist.

At midnight, there was a gentle knock on Sage's door. She opened it and let Elem in.

CHAPTER TWENTY FOUR

"I hope we still get breakfast," Sage said, smiling contentedly.

"Of course we do, though it must be a quick one. We are required to be ready to disembark at ten o'clock," Morgan stated. "Is everyone packed?"

"All I need to do is empty the safe of my jewelry," Sage said.

"All I need to do is finish that last bottle of champagne," Jon burped.

Peter arrived promptly at nine thirty in the morning with a cart for the luggage.

"I'm sorry to see you go. These short cruises don't give us enough time to truly get to know our guests, which is a shame," he lamented. "I do believe your final bill was left under your door during the night for you to examine. If all is agreed, I need only your signature."

Morgan returned a copy of the bill, with her signature at the bottom. "It has been our pleasure, Peter. You've made our short stay quite pleasant," she said, handing him a well-padded plain envelope.

"Thank you, madam, and I took the liberty of contacting the limo service and your driver should be waiting for you."

As the four made their way down the gangplank, Sage paused. Then she turned around and looked up to see Elem watching her from the third deck railing. She smiled at him and laying her hand on her heart, turned away.

"Well, that was a most delightful diversion!" Lyle exclaimed. "In all my years, I've never been on a cruise. Thank you so much for including us."

Sage had retrieved their keys from the lock box and handed them out again, leaving the spares on the table as before. "We were only gone two days yet it feels like longer."

"That's because the days, and nights, were full," Lyle added. "What do we do now?"

"I'm going to find a nice shady spot to read for the afternoon," Sage said. She took her case and hung her clothes up, pausing at the red dress.

The foursome left the rental unit at seven in the evening to find a place for dinner.

"As much as I've enjoyed the local foods over the last few days, I think I would like something simple like a hamburger and fries," Morgan announced. And so it was decided they would go back to Margaritaville for a casual and relaxing evening.

They returned, tired and happy, at midnight.

At one o'clock in the morning, Morgan was suddenly awake, disturbed by an unknown presence nearby. She rose silently and stood by her closed door to listen. She opened her senses and listened to every small sound. She heard Sage breathing softly in the next room, and Jon roll over in his sleep, and…something else: Footsteps. She opened the door without a sound. Before she stepped forward,

Morgan remembered that part of the floor creaked and levitated only enough to pass the warped board.

A shadow passed by the entrance to the kitchen where just enough moonlight shone in to outline a small tight body.

That someone would invade their privacy angered Morgan and she lashed out with a bolt of blue energy, slamming the person against the far wall. She held them there while she magically turned on all the lights.

The noise of the intruder's capture woke the household. Sage was the first one by Morgan's side, and soon Lyle and Jon were sleepily stumbling down the stairs.

With all the lights on, it was easy for them all to see a petite body covered head to toe in black Lycra, feet dangled above the floor.

"Now what do we have here?" Morgan said with a sneer. "A cat-burglar?" she walked closer and yanked the hood and head gear off, exposing a very-frightened, dark face with blond hair.

"What is that?" Sage asked, looking at the strange contraption.

"I do believe those are infrared night goggles: a sure way of getting around in the dark without tripping," Morgan replied.

"So how did he get in? I know the doors were locked; I checked them myself," Lyle said.

"Yes, and did you notice the French doors to our balcony are open now," Jon commented. "I bet he opened them so it would be a quick escape if we woke up while he was rifling through our things!"

That's when Sage noticed the pile of items on the dining room table, and a key, much like theirs. "It would appear he has his own key. So much for the coded lock box security." She got closer to look at the items and gasped. "I know this was in my room," she sneered picking up her ruby necklace. "You're nothing but a petty thief with the gall to come into an occupied room. You'll pay for this." She got up close to him and said, "You almost made the score of a lifetime, but you picked the wrong people to steal from." Her anger simmered a fraction below her control and tears formed in her eyes. She slipped the necklace into her robe pocket and backed away, breathing heavy.

"That's the last time I take that ring off!" Jon and Lyle retrieved their wedding bands from the pile.

"What do you think we should do with him?" Morgan asked. The flickering blue pulse expanded and he was picked up another foot. His eyes grew wide in fear.

"Where did you get the key?" Jon finally spoke, his voice low and menacing was met with silence. "I asked you a question!"

"You will tell us," Morgan spoke softly and the energy pouring from her hand increased and heated. The burglar squirmed in pain. She backed off the intensity and spun him upside down.

"You're not going to kill him, are you?" Sage asked.

"No, at least not yet," Morgan got a sly grin on her face.

"Where did you get the key?" Lyle joined in, repeating Jon's question.

"From...from...Alfred," the small man confessed. "He always picks the target."

"Our congenial host set this up? Interesting." Morgan held her hand out and slowly curled her fingers into a fist, pushing the energy deeper into his chest and the burglar felt the beginning of a heart attack and moaned in agony. She released him then snapped her fingers and the man was out cold and she dropped him to the floor. "Find something to tie him up with while I call the constable."

Twenty minutes later, red and blue flashing lights arrived at the curb.

"And that's what he told us before he passed out, likely from fear that he had finally been caught," Lyle said.

The police officer poured cold water over the perp's face until he woke. As soon as he opened his eyes, he scooted away. "Keep her away from me! She used voodoo on me!"

"Me?" Morgan laughed. "What a ridiculous tale. Do you need

us to come in and make a statement, sir?" she politely asked the police.

"No, ma'am. No need to come in; he's been caught red-handed this time. We've had other complaints in the past about break-ins here. This bust will solve a number of open cases," Officer Jenkins closed his notebook, thinking two thieves dealt with in one week made for a good ending.

"Get some rest, kids, we're leaving in the morning," Morgan said heading back to bed.

"Leaving?" Sage questioned.

"I'm sorry dear, I've had enough of this place." She paused. "Truthfully, Sage, I was so angry I almost hurt that man. I could have easily killed him; I *wanted* to kill him and that distresses me."

"Do we really have to leave?" Jon pouted.

Morgan looked at the two men, her two best friends, and realized it wasn't fair to cut their vacation short even by two or three days.

"No, you two don't need to leave. Stay here, the lease is paid in full, though I doubt Mr. Picard is in any position to protest; your fishing trip tomorrow is already paid too. And Lyle, I'm sure you still have my debit card, so use it if you need to, and I'll leave you the flight plans and tickets. Enjoy yourselves, but Sage and I are leaving." She saw the white cat circling Sage's ankles. "And it looks like we will need to take the private jet back to Manhattan, so Paws can come too."

CHAPTER TWENTY FIVE

"**W**elcome home, Miss Morgan," Henry said, relieving the limo driver of the bags. "We didn't expect you back for a few more days." Heavy midafternoon traffic delayed their arrival until after five o'clock.

Paws jumped down from Sage's arms and sniffed at Henry's shoes.

"And who is this new guest?"

"This is Paws, a Hemingway cat and a new member of our household," Morgan announced. "I called the twenty-four-hour grocery on our way back. Cat food and litter should arrive shortly. Please make sure that Alyce puts those items on her regular shopping list." Morgan clenched her hands together to keep them from shaking. "We'll have dinner in the library in an hour, and I realize we were unexpected, so whatever Alyce can come up with will be fine. Sage, please come with me."

Behind the closed doors of the library, Morgan finally let go of her hands. They sought out the nearest object, an ornate vase, and smashed the expensive vessel into the fireplace.

Sage stood very still.

"I'm having some difficulty controlling my anger, it would seem. Better to break a vase that I never really liked, than to break that crook's neck!"

"Red or white?" Sage asked calmly, making her way to the newly installed, dual-sided wine refrigerator.

"Both," Morgan said and barked out a laugh that was half sob.

Sage opened a chardonnay and a California red blend and set four glasses on the sideboard with the bottles. She poured Morgan a glass from each bottle and a glass of red for herself, and she waited.

"I know you've been with me for only six months, Sage. I feel we've gotten very close in that short time. Close enough that I can now tell you things about myself and about my past; things that no one else knows. Are you ready for that burden?"

"Friends don't consider...confidences a burden," Sage answered with a wisdom that initially surprised Morgan.

"Now this may seem strange, and please don't take it personally, but as I start talking about this, which I've never done before, I'm likely to get angry and start throwing things again. So I'm asking you to stay over there, and I'm putting a protective shield around you. I wouldn't want you to accidently get hurt by flying debris," Morgan said, sadness laced her voice.

"Deal. I think I'll open another bottle of red though, so we each have one," Sage smiled. "Can I ask questions?"

"Yes, though I might not answer immediately," Morgan said. "Is there something in particular you want to know?"

"Who is Evon?" Sage asked carefully, taking a bottle of wine to her side of the invisible shield. *Nearly* invisible, she could see a light shimmer of blue in the air.

Morgan seemed to slump. "He was my brother." She took a deep breath and continued. "Our mother, Haedre, was not our birth mother, and even though Evon wasn't born my brother we were raised together as siblings. Same as I searched for you, Haedre searched for us.

"She was the most powerful sorceress ever and approaching a thousand years old. She wanted to finally rest, to die, but not before she trained her apprentice. In our case, two of us. We were to balance each other. When she found I had been born on 12-21-1221, she stole me from my home. I was two years old. Then she found Evon, who was born on 6-21-1221, she took him too: The winter solstice and the summer; male and female; a blue eyed blond, and one with dark hair, dark eyes. We were complete opposites in every way.

"Haedre raised us in magic. She taught us spells and chants; she taught us how to call down the power from the sky, and to call up the power from the earth, and in from the sea; most of all, she taught us how to call up the power within ourselves.

"It was all we knew. It was all we *needed* to know. By the time we were teens, we were both quite accomplished in the arts. I was always into mischief and Evon was always quietly helping someone: Opposites. We celebrated our birthday together on September 21, the Autumnal Equinox. We were to be equals, but we weren't. Evon's goodness made him stronger, and that made me jealous.

"On our eighteenth birthday, Haedre presented us with our star stones as you see them now, on the neck of an enchanted serpent. She explained how the stones worked, and she told us of our births—that we were not brother and sister as we thought, and that she had chosen us to be mates. The idea appalled Evon, and his blatant rejection angered me.

"That night, Haedre died. I took a bottle of wine to Evon's chambers to tell him, got him drunk, and then I seduced him. When he realized what he had done, he threw me out of his bed and wept until he fell asleep. That's when I took his star stone and put a spell on him.

"He would walk the earth as a mortal, never knowing how powerful he once had been. He would die a mortal and reincarnate as a mortal, again and again, until the day he found someone to love him for himself, and then he would begin to remember. The side effect of the spell I used is that *I* would not only never find love myself, but I would also never recognize his soul, his aura, to break the spell and ask his forgiveness."

Morgan stopped, took a long drink of the red wine, and threw the empty glass into the burning fireplace where it shattered casting prisms of light dancing off the walls.

"Once I had my stone, his stone, and Haedre's staff which contained the third stone, I was unstoppable. I was easily offended back then and I grew meaner with each passing year and my power continued to grow.

"I would find some man that appealed to me and I would cast a love spell on him. It didn't matter if he was married or how old or young he was, if I wanted him he was *mine*. I used him until I got bored and then cast him away, his life in ruins. I didn't care. I did it again and again over my life time. Until I met someone I actually cared about."

A gentle knock on the door pulled Morgan from her reverie. A quick snap of her fingers lowered the shield around Sage, and Henry wheeled in their dinner. He put the cart next to the table, spread a pink linen cloth over the small table, set it with napkins and silverware, and then he departed, all without a word.

"Hmm, Cornish hens stuffed with rice pilaf and a Caesar salad," Sage said. "You should give Alyce a raise. Likely, this is her and Henry's dinner." They ate in silence a few minutes before Morgan spoke.

"In the morning, after we are both rested, you're going back again."

Sage paused with her fork halfway to her mouth. "To when?" she asked, putting her fork down without eating that morsel.

"I'm trying something more defined this time, by focusing on a particular year and place: The fall of 1692, Massachusetts."

Sage looked scared. "The Salem witch trials? Why?"

"You need to find me."

"Wasn't Salem a risky place for you to be?" Sage questioned.

"It wasn't when I first arrived."

Sage raised her eyebrows in a silent question.

"Who do you think started it all?' Morgan said. "You need to stop me."

CHAPTER TWENTY SIX

---◆◆◆---

"**Y**ou know, as much as I love Morgan and Sage, these last two days alone have been the best part of the vacation," Jon commented, pouring a second cup of coffee.

"Yes, but it concerns me that Morgan rushed off like she did. She dealt with that thief before any of us knew what was happening, why would she be so upset? Nothing can harm her."

"I wish I knew the answer to that." Jon was interrupted by a knock on the door. Elem Houser stood pacing on the wide porch when Lyle cautiously opened the door.

"Can we help you?" Jon said from behind Lyle.

"I sure hope so. You were on the cruise ship...with Sage," Elem said nervously. "I have to see her. Is she here?"

"No, they went back to New York two days ago," Jon said, warranting an elbow from Lyle for divulging too much information.

"New York? Where in New York?"

"You're that dance instructor! Why do you want to see Sage?"

"Ever since she left the ship, I haven't been able to get her out of my mind. I know this sounds crazy coming from a man of my age, but..." Elem hesitated, "I love her, and I'm sure she feels the same. I feel as if I've known her for a lifetime—more than a lifetime. Please, this is the most important thing that has ever happened in my life; help me find her."

"When you say you've known her for more than a lifetime, what do you mean?" Lyle asked cautiously. He knew that Sage had been in the past and had met a man she was falling in love with when she was snapped back to the present. Morgan assured them, all of them, that reincarnation was a fact, not a myth, and that some people remembered snippets of their previous lives. And even though most did not, people often brought forward talents and knowledge without understanding where it came from.

"I don't know if this will make any sense, but when we danced, when I held her in my arms, it felt as if we had done that before. When I saw her in that blue dress with the blue crystal, I felt I was repeating something that had already happened, and when she wore the ruby necklace, it was as if I had seen that too, but not on her. I swear the ship's deck tilted, and I felt dizzy," Elem confessed, looking as disheveled and distraught as he felt.

Jon stood there, his mouth hanging open. He stared at Elem for a moment and then said, "Excuse us," and he shut the door on the man, pulling Lyle in with him.

"Are you thinking what I'm thinking?" Lyle asked.

"That this Elem is Ethan from the *Titanic*? Oh, yeah. Remember, that ruby necklace was part of his family for a long time, and Helen was wearing it the first night Ethan met Sage. The question now is what are we going to do?"

"If they are meant to be together, we can't stand in their way."

"Elem," Lyle said, "How would you like to come to New York with us? We just happen to have an extra ticket."

CHAPTER TWENTY SEVEN

------------------- ❊ -------------------

Morgan called for a cab and was whisked away before Sage woke. By her usual *luck*, Morgan's attorney happened to have an opening to see her immediately. Remembering her last visit with him, she began to age herself while she rode the empty elevator to the 21st floor of the high-rise office building. She emerged looking the appropriate age of eighty-five, leaning heavy on her staff.

"Nice to see you again, Mrs. Alsteen. Please, have a seat. What can I do for you?" Floyd Astrape said, smiling widely. Before she arrived, he took the time to look up her previous visit over five years ago. She was a very wealthy woman and had made some changes to her will *and* had paid her bill promptly, a bonus to any business.

"I need to make a few revisions to my will," she said. Although her voice had aged too, it was still strong and commanding.

"I thought that might be the case, so I took the liberty to pull out a copy of your previous will." He handed her a copy and opened his. "Now, what changes would you like to make?"

Morgan said, "I'd like to increase the endowments to Henry, Alyce, Lyle and Jon."

"An easy adjustment. Anything else?"

"Yes, I'd like to add Miss Sage Aster as my primary beneficiary," Morgan stated. "She is to get the real estate properties and all the contents. Also, the stocks I have listed in my assets. Then, she is to get whatever monies remain after the endowments and the settlement fees."

"May I ask what her relationship is to you?" Floyd questioned. He had seen too many times someone new had inserted themselves into the life of an older person to get into their will.

"No, you may not. The relationship is irrelevant. Here is her identification card; take a copy of it, so you personally can verify her identity when I pass," Morgan said. "I understand you're looking out for me, Mr. Astrape, and I appreciate that. Rest assured though, this is not what you may think. In fact, I suggest you do a background check on her to ease your conscious…and add it to my bill."

"May I ask how your health is?"

"My health is excellent, Mr. Astrape. How is yours?" she asked with a smirk.

"I'm asking only to know how quickly this needs to be done, ma'am."

"Actually, since I'm aware this is all kept on your computer, and that these changes are relatively minor, I intend to wait while you complete the task. I dislike coming into the city these days, almost as much as I dislike having company," she quickly added, to discourage him from offering to bring the new will to her at home.

"May I bring you a cup of coffee while I tend to this, Mrs. Alsteen?"

Since Morgan had left the house early, Sage had a light breakfast of coffee and cinnamon toast in the atrium among the flowers she had grown to love. She clipped a few drooping buds, discarding them into the compost pile, then cut a single white sweetheart rose for the tiny green vase in her bathroom.

"Oh, there you are," Sage greeted Morgan as she came in the

front door. "Had I known you were going into the city I would have gotten up in time to go with you."

"Not a problem, dear, it was a private errand. Have you had lunch yet? I left without eating, and I'm ready for a big meal," Morgan said. The energy burned to keep changing or holding her appearance, as always, used many calories that needed to be replenished.

"I had some toast and coffee over an hour ago. Would you like me to have Alyce fix us something?"

"Yes, you need to eat something more substantial. You leave in an hour." Morgan turned to her rooms and stopped at Sage's gasp. "Don't worry, it will be fine."

After putting the sealed envelope with the new will on the desk in her room, where it could be easily found if someone were looking for it, Morgan went to the sunroom off the greeting room, where she and Sage had been dining since the warmer weather returned.

Sage wheeled in a cart, laden with two thick roast beef sandwiches, cups of soup, and a bowl of potato salad. Henry made sure the table was always pre-set for them, enabling Sage to serve Morgan immediately.

Sage picked at her food.

"Eat!" Morgan commanded. "Look, Sage, I don't know exactly what time of day you will arrive in the past and there sure isn't any take-out where you're going. Besides, if memory serves me, the food back then wasn't that good and there wasn't much of it, so you need to eat."

Sage picked up her spoon and finished the chunky tomato soup. She ate half of the huge sandwich and added potato salad to her plate.

"What about clothes? Shouldn't we wait until Lyle comes back?" Sage said, hoping to stall the inevitable.

"Having him outfit you for the last trip was to make him feel useful. I can adjust anything you chose to wear, to make it fit the era."

"Are you sure you'll get it right?"

"You forget I *lived* that time," Morgan snapped with a touch of anger at being challenged.

"Morgan, I'm sorry...I'm just nervous. I certainly didn't mean to offend you," Sage said in deep sincerity. "Should I wear a long skirt, or perhaps go as a boy?" It saddened and frightened her to have Morgan angry at her.

"Find a long dark skirt, a dark or gray long sleeved blouse, and a hat. I can change the structure of what you choose, I can't materialize it. I believe Lyle replaced your boots, those would be good." While Sage was upstairs changing, Morgan went to what Sage had dubbed the magic room, and practiced deep breathing exercises to refocus and center herself. It was getting more and more difficult to keep control. Time was running out.

Sage returned wearing a slim black skirt, a dark-green blouse, and carrying a baseball cap. "I brought a shawl along too. Will I need it?"

"The shawl was a good idea. Stand in the circle, please." Morgan took her staff and tapped it on the floor. It wobbled slightly then stood by itself. She removed the serpent from her wrist, put it around Sage's neck, and stepped back. A pass of her hand changed the black slim skirt into a dark-gray full skirt of coarse material; another pass turned the green shirt a lighter gray and the baseball cap into a white day cap with long tails ending under the chin. Yet another pass turned the shawl into a woolen cape.

Sage looked down at her clothes in amazement. "I will never doubt you again, Morgan. I do have a question though. If by chance something is left behind, will it revert to its original features?"

"I don't know, so try not to lose anything to be on the safe side. We certainly don't want a baseball cap showing up in the history books," Morgan chuckled. She retrieved the staff and began drawing the lines of fire. "Just remember…"

"I know, go with the flow." She crouched down to keep from getting dizzy upon landing.

A final pass of Morgan's hand and Sage disappeared.

CHAPTER TWENTY EIGHT

The full moon was bright and high in the sky when Sage appeared in 1692. The stars shone more spectacular than she remembered ever seeing, realizing there was no pollution here to block the night sky. Even though the air was seasonably pleasant, she pulled the wool cape around her tighter, more for comfort than for warmth. She looked around cautiously, using the brilliance of the moon to get her bearings. Even so, without artificial light all she could make out were shapes and shadows.

She could tell most of what she could see were houses or at least buildings of some kind, and since no candlelight came from within them, she guessed it was the middle of the night and everyone was asleep. Stepping carefully, Sage came upon a larger building with a distinctive shadow and looked up. The big moon hung slightly to the east of a cross on top of the structure. She'd found a church, a sanctuary for the night. She hoped.

Sage did not allow herself to sleep, and at first dawn, which was not much brighter than the full moon, she silently eased her way out of the musty church, and made her way to what appeared to be the edge of town. During the night, she thought it might be better to seem as if she was just arriving in town. Then what? She thought.

Would Morgan be known by her real name or would she have an alias? No, Morgan had a great deal of pride; she would never use an alias, and if she did, she would have told Sage.

As the day brightened, and all too quickly, Sage found a high spot behind a thin copse of leafy trees to watch from. The town square, such as it was, was centered around a large, common stone faced well that soon became the focus of the early morning activity. People, mostly women, came and went, carrying heavy buckets of water. Pulling together all of her courage, she ventured down the hill and made to approach from the road.

"Good morn, gentle women," she greeted the six women gathered around the open well. They looked up from their task in terror of the stranger. "Oh please, do not fear me. I'm only from Suffolk and I come seeking my sister. Perhaps you know of her and can guide me to her dwelling. Her name is Morgan." One of the women fainted. The rest backed up a step.

"My goodness! Is she ill? Perhaps she hasn't broken fast as of yet and is weak," Sage offered, wondering if the mention of Morgan's name caused this. "Come, a little cool water on her face should help." One of the older women ventured forward with her bucket and splashed some water on the prone woman who quickly woke up. Sage helped her stand when the other women refused.

"I ask again, can you tell me where to find my sister?"

The women stayed silent.

Sage let out a sigh. "I find it distressing that my widowed sister would find refuge in what she thought to be such a godly village when it seems that the folk will not answer a simple question from an innocent stranger." She intentionally looked up at the church steeple to make her point. "Good day. I will ask someone else." She turned to walk away.

"She lives a short walk outside of town. The dwelling with the pretty flowers and prosperous vegetables," the same older woman said, pointing the way Sage had come.

"I thank you, madam," Sage straightened her shoulders and lifted her chin as though she was still affronted, when in fact she was relieved that Morgan was here and close by.

Five minutes of walking along the dusty road, the way she had come, Sage saw her. Morgan had a bucket in her hand and was coming right toward her.

"Morgan!" she increased her pace to reach her sooner.

Morgan looked up, her dark eyes guarded. "Do I know you, child?"

"Not yet, but you will." Sage smiled at the familiar endearment. "Let me carry that bucket for you. Were you going for water? I'll get it for you. And please, Morgan, those women at the well think... um...I told them you were my sister. It was the only way they would tell me where to find you and quite reluctantly I may add. We really have to talk."

"You speak quite oddly. We are rife with witches that have entered the village, are you one of them? Should I be afraid of you?" Morgan spoke with the cadence of the time.

"You aren't afraid of anyone, Morgan, and I know who—and what—you are," Sage took the chance and let the star stone out from behind the high-necked shirt.

Morgan stopped and stared. "Who are you?"

"Let's get your water and go back to your house to talk in private." Sage looped her arm through Morgan's and kept her walking. Morgan was too stunned to resist.

"Good morn, gentle women," Morgan greeted those who remained at the well. They looked down and backed away. Sage took the bucket and looked into the well, wondering how she pulled up water.

"Are you simple minded, child?" Morgan lowered a bucket that was securely attached to a rope, pulled up the water and poured it into her empty one.

"Sorry, I've never had to do this before, but I'm a fast learner." Sage lowered the pail again and was able to fill their bucket fully.

———◦❈◦———

"Why are those women so afraid of you?" Sage asked carrying the heavy bucket now filled with the clean well water back to Morgan's small house.

"If you truly know who I am you wouldn't be asking such foolish questions." Morgan walked into the house, letting the door shut on Sage, who kicked it open with a snarl. "Put the water by the stove, then get out!"

"I'm not leaving until we talk, Morgan. *You* were the one who sent me here, so talk we will!" Sage shot back.

"Me? I've never laid eyes on you before, child. I did not send for you. Now leave me!"

"No!" Sage stood her ground. "Your future self sent me here, because you have turned into a mean and hateful bitch, and it's affecting her, you, in her time. Does that make any sense?"

"Are you saying I've perfected traveling back in time?" Morgan asked quietly. "If that is what you claim, then why didn't I come myself? I would be more apt to believe me than you."

"As you explained it to me, you can't travel to a time when you already exist. Both of you can't be in the same time-space. One of you would cease to be, and since the future Morgan is more powerful, then *you* would cease, and if you ceased to be so would she." Sage sat on a hard chair.

"That does sound reasonable, *if* I were to believe you." Morgan asked, putting the tips of her fingers together. "How can I be sure you are not a council informant trying to trap me into a confession for witchcraft?"

"Well, you're not a witch; you're a sorceress, and you are over four hundred years old. Witches don't live that long," Sage stated.

"How did you know that?" Morgan stood, alarmed.

"I keep trying to tell you, *you* told me all this." Sage sighed. "Wait, you've been accused of witchcraft? So, you've been working magic on these people? Maybe that's what you should stop doing."

"Why should I stop? These people are simpletons, and they amuse me. And now that you've claimed to be my sister, the magistrate will be after you too," Morgan laughed.

"So you're hurting innocent people for amusement? That doesn't sound like the Morgan I know," Sage scowled.

Someone pounded on the door.

Morgan tilted her head and smiled. "An elder and the handsome William have come to call. They can't see you here. Be gone, I wish to see William alone!"

"I'm not going anywhere. You told me once that a concealment spell was one of the most basic—so conceal me!"

The knock came louder.

"Sit on that chair in the corner and be quiet!" Morgan waved her hands and Sage was behind...something.

Sage looked around. She could still see the entire room, though there felt to be a force-field of sorts distorting her vision. Maybe it was the energy of the concealment spell. She sat and stayed still and watched two men enter the room. One was old, short, and portly, while the other was tall and quite attractive.

"Good day to you, Proctor, and to you, William," Morgan smiled seductively at the tall one. "What brings you here to my humble home?"

"We hear you have a visitor—your sister? We will question her about causing Abagail to faint this morn at the well," the older one said.

"As you can see, Proctor, there is no one here aside from myself, and you've already questioned me and found me innocent, haven't you?" Morgan lifted her hands in supplication, casting a spell for the old man to agree with anything she said. Through the veil of the concealment, Sage could see a faint blue energy emanating from Morgan's hands.

"Yes, yes, of course Mistress Alsteen, my mistake. Come William," he turned to the door in a daze.

"William wishes to stay for a visit and a cup of tea, don't you William?" Morgan pushed his mind with hers.

"A cup of tea would be most welcome," he said.

Another spell cast. Sage thought he looked confused and would likely do anything she wants. She had seen Morgan do this before.

The one named Proctor walked out and closed the door without saying another word. William stood silently.

"How is your wife, William? I heard she is doing poorly," Morgan said sweetly with fake concern.

"Yes, she has not been herself for many weeks now. She says things I do not understand and wishes to be alone all the time," William replied.

"That must be very difficult for you. A man must have his *needs* taken care of, and if a wife doesn't share her bed with him, he can become ill." Morgan slowly walked around him, touching his arm, then shoulder until she stood in front and very close to him.

"It's been a long time since I've shared my bed, William. I could take care of your needs," Morgan reached up and kissed him. He clutched her to him and returned her kiss passionately.

"Morgan!" Sage called out from behind the concealment spell. "Don't do it!" William heard a cat meow and stopped. A white cat, with a golden collar and blue stone sat on a chair in the corner.

Morgan snapped her fingers and William froze. "I told you to be quiet! You're ruining everything!" she snarled.

"Release him. This isn't what you want. *He* isn't who you want."

"And who do I want?" Morgan's anger was building.

"Evon."

"How…."

"Release William, and send him back to his wife, and I'll tell you more," Sage bargained.

CHAPTER TWENTY NINE

———————————•❋•———————————

"**H**ow do you know about Evon?" Anger flashed in Morgan's dark eyes. "No one knows about him, and I've never told anyone."

"The future you told me about him. The spell you cast on him is affecting you too. You will never find real love until you break that spell. All these men that come to you, Morgan, don't really love you, and you don't love them either, do you? You use them and cast them aside, their lives destroyed by your magic. Did you cast a spell on William's wife too, to make her act strange, so you could get close to him and satisfy your lust? That will make two lives destroyed at one time.

"And you didn't really want Evon either, you wanted his power. You got his star stone, but you didn't get his power, did you? His power came from his goodness and that made him strong. Until you end this destructive course you're on, you will never be as strong as him. Do the village of Salem a kindness, Morgan, and release all of those under your magic. I can't undo history; however, *you* can keep more from happening."

Morgan rested her head on her arms and took deep breaths. "Bending people to my will brings me pleasure, and the power to do that is intoxicating. It will be difficult to end. I'm not sure I *want* that to end," she said, looking up with a sneer.

"Replace the evil, selfish spells with good ones then. Good deeds can be equally satisfying," Sage sat again. "Say, did you turn me into a cat?"

"Only William's perception of you was a cat. When you spoke, he heard a meow; when you continued, the concealment spell started to crumble." Morgan stood to pace. She picked up the bucket of water and set it on a small table near the woodstove. "I will ask you questions and you will answer them." She waved her hand at Sage.

"Your spells won't work on me, Morgan. I think the star stone prevents that. Ask me whatever you want, and I will do my best to answer. However, there are things you aren't meant to know yet."

"I dislike that answer," Morgan poured water into a kettle and set it on the stove that she lit with a point of her finger. "What time are you from?" She asked, hoping to catch Sage off balance.

"About four hundred years from now," Sage said with a frown. "The year is now 2021."

Morgan's eyes widened. "I live to be eight hundred? Am I well?"

"Yes, for the most part, I think. You have maintained your appearance, and everyone believes you to be as you look today, perhaps thirty years old—which is young to us. The average life span is past eighty years now."

"You hesitated, child. What are you not telling me?" Morgan pressed.

Sage turned to fully face her. "You seem to have a short fuse lately."

"Fuse? What is a fuse?" Morgan looked perplexed.

"Sorry, let me rephrase that. You are quick to anger is the best way to describe it. We were recently somewhere, and a thief came into our rooms; you almost killed him," Sage said recalling the incident.

"It sounds as though he would have deserved to die," Morgan said matter-of-factly.

"Our society is much different from...now. We don't kill because someone steals, or offends us, or harms us. That isn't the point though, Morgan. There is something happening with the you of the future that you aren't sharing with me."

"Is that all? That I am quick to anger? I don't see the problem."

"It isn't only that. You seem...weak. You're having more and more difficulty walking and after you do, you need to rest longer and longer. There are many little things that remain little, so it's difficult to explain especially since you think I don't notice." Sage recalled Morgan's hands shaking and the other unwarranted outbursts, but kept quiet. "All I know is that in the future you sent me back here to change something concerning you, and I don't know what that is, but it's killing her...and you."

"Would it be safe for us to walk around the town? I've read many things about Salem, things I would like to see for myself," Sage suggested, getting them off the subject of the future. She knew there was much she couldn't tell this Morgan, for fear of changing future events.

They stepped outside into a cool wind.

"Ah, there will be rain this afternoon. The gardens need the water," Morgan said casually.

"The woman at the well said your garden was the most prosperous. May I see it?"

"They are only vegetables. I use some of them to trade for other things I want like eggs, or wine, or bread. The trading is easy," Morgan smiled. "Their gardens don't do as well as mine does, so mine are in demand." She chuckled.

"Are you keeping them from having enough food?" Sage said tightly.

"Only certain vegetables are growing better here. They still grow many root crops which keep them fed. If only *my* garden did well, it would bring too much attention to me. My above ground plants do better than theirs," she smiled knowingly, "and then there are the flowers they have extreme difficulty with. The women love pretty things, and their men come to me for a blossom or two. Let's pick some flowers, and a few tomatoes. I know who will gladly give me eggs for them." Morgan snipped off several large blossoms of zinnia-like flowers and Sage watched as new blossoms instantly grew to replace them.

Sage set the flowers, two large red tomatoes, and a cucumber in the flat basket Morgan furnished, and they walked the short distance into town along the rutted and dusty road.

As they neared the well where several women were standing, one of the women set a toddler up on the edge of the stonework to re-tie her bonnet. A crack of thunder overhead caused one of the women to jump back in surprise, bumping into the other woman who jostled the child and caused the toddler to fall into the well. The woman screamed.

Sage and Morgan rushed to peer over the edge and saw the young girl struggling in the water. The mother wailed in anguish as she too watched.

"Save her, Morgan!" Sage hissed quietly.

"Why?"

"Because you *can*, that's why!" Sage tossed the water bucket into the deep well hoping the child would grab hold, as she watched the youngster's struggles diminish. Morgan frowned as she leaned over the edge, and levitated the child into the bucket.

Sage straightened and said, "Help me!" she handed the end of the rope to another woman standing there and together they pulled the child to safety.

With the wet little girl in her arms again, the mother wept with joy. "Thank you, thank you! You saved Sarah's life!" she said to Sage.

"Not I, though I am pleased the child is rescued. This gentle woman pulled much harder than I. Mayhap someone so young should not sit on the well edge." Sage turned away, picked up the basket she had dropped, and she and Morgan made their way through the crowd that was forming.

When they were away from the crowd, Sage leaned closer to Morgan and whispered, "Now didn't that feel good? You saved a life."

"They know not that it was I who did that."

"Exactly. Doing things without being praised is the best kind of good deed. Besides, do you *want* them to know?"

"No, I do not. They would either want me to do more, or they would try to hang me as a witch!"

Morgan made her delivery of flowers and vegetables, and collected her payment of six fresh eggs then insisted they avoid the town square.

"I still do not understand the desire to do these good deeds," Morgan continued to protest while leading them on a winding trek.

"Look at it this way: it takes more power to do something that others cannot see, than to do it openly. Plus, it's good karma. I think Evon understood this," Sage said, knowing she was venturing into sore subjects. Morgan remained silent.

"What is in this direction?" Sage questioned, being unfamiliar with the real-time town.

"Over there is where the gallows have been put up to hang the convicted witches," Morgan said casually.

"Gallows Hill?" Sage gasped. "I think I'd rather we avoid that. There must be so much sadness that lingers there."

"Tell me more about your travels through time, Sage," Morgan pressed. She had picked a carrot, a turnip and an onion to add to the pot cooking on the stove and was cleaning them in some water.

"Each time I travel, there is something I need to fix and when I accomplish that, I go back to my time. I don't always know what that is though. In fact, I never know what I'm supposed to do at first. Once I was in my past for a little more than a day, another time two weeks," Sage looked away, remembering.

"How is it you can go to your past, and I can't" Morgan asked.

"The time I go back to was before I was born, so I'm not there. You, on the other hand, have lived so long that you are always there, somewhere. Besides it's *your* deeds that need changing now," Sage explained. "What are you fixing? Can I help?"

"It is only a stew," Morgan sighed. "A stew I'm getting tired of."

"Let me make some pasta to go with it," Sage offered.

"What is pasta?"

Sage took the cutting board and piled some flour in the center. She made a well in the middle, and then took two of the fresh eggs, a small amount of melted lard, a pinch of precious salt and some water and after mixing them together, poured the mixture into the center and started blending in the flour. She rolled it out and cut long strips and then crosswise into smaller pieces, dropping it all into boiling water.

Morgan watched as Sage put some of the cooked pasta into two bowls and then ladled the stew on top. Sage used a spoon to scoop the concoction into her mouth. Morgan followed suit, and her eyes widened at the wonderful taste and texture of the new food.

"I think I like having you around, Sage-from-the-future. What other new foods can you make?"

"How many tomatoes can you spare?"

---—--●--—---

"Morgan, have you been putting spells on the young girls in town and causing them to act strangely and then having them accuse the older women of witchcraft?" Sage asked as she cleared the table of their early supper. It was September and the nights were arriving earlier and earlier. Knowing candles were scarce, Sage was preparing herself for an early bed time, which was fine since she hadn't slept since she arrived.

"And if I have, what is the harm?"

"Harm? Are you kidding me? Innocent women are dying, being hung for something they didn't do!" Sage exclaimed. "You must stop this, Morgan. Hurting others is bad for your soul."

CHAPTER THIRTY

---✦---

Sage stretched her back. Sleeping on the floor was not her first choice, and she ended up with a crick in her lower back. She had volunteered to sleep near the stove and keep it going throughout the night during the thunder storm. Now she made some biscuits, added water to the kettle, and started it heating for tea while Morgan slept in.

Morgan had been enthused after dinner that she was to get yet another new meal to try, and told Sage she could take as many tomatoes and onions as she needed. Introducing spaghetti into the seventeenth century might not be the wisest thing, however Sage went on her gut feeling that it wouldn't matter. Maybe this was the beginning of Morgan's expanded palette and that's all.

---✦---

Sage stepped out into the foggy morning. The rain during the night still clung to the leaves on the trees and dripped into the puddles that had formed on the parched road; the sun glistened behind the still present clouds offering a gray smudge in the sky. Sage took a deep breath of the clean air and smiled even though she also got a whiff of the outhouse. *The privy,* she corrected herself.

She carefully picked six tomatoes, some garlic, and two onions from the garden to start the tomato sauce for an all-day simmer. Herbs could be added later, if Morgan had any.

Before she could get back into the house, Sage heard voices and ducked behind a large shrub to watch. In their long dark skirts, pale gray blouses and white bonnets, four women and two young girls were coming down the road, all of them carrying baskets full of clothes. After they passed, Sage slipped into the house unnoticed.

"Where would the women be going with baskets of clothes?" she asked Morgan who had risen and was now making tea.

"Likely they are going down to the river to wash and bathe."

"Bathe? That sounds like a wonderful idea. Can we go too?"

"If you wish, however first we must break our nightly fast," Morgan looked at the table where Sage set a plate full of biscuits she had made earlier. "You've been busy this morn, Sage-from-the-future. Do you cook for me then too?"

"No, you have servants to do that and everything else."

"Servants? Am I a wealthy woman?" Morgan smiled, pleased at the thought.

"Yes, you are quite wealthy. You also have friends that visit often, and you have me. I live in the house with you," Sage commented. "Sit and have a biscuit or two with your tea."

"I have friends? Interesting." Morgan said softly. She never had a friend, didn't have any now, except for this strange girl from the future.

Sage and Morgan went further upstream from where the other women were rinsing their heavy skirts in the river water. There were wet dresses, aprons, men's trousers, and shirts hanging from branches and shrubs. The women and girls themselves were wading or sitting in the shallows, splashing the warm water on themselves and each other.

Sage stepped out of her long skirt, and pulled off her blouse. After rinsing the blouse in the water, she hung it to dry across a bush. Just before she stepped into the water, she looked at Morgan.

"What's the matter?"

"You are...nearly naked! And what is it you're wearing?" Morgan gasped.

Sage looked down at her knee length bloomers and camisole. "In my time, Morgan, these are never worn. In fact, I feel silly wearing this much."

"Help!" someone screamed out.

Sage looked around some shrubs growing at the water's edge to downstream and saw one of the younger girls floundering in the water, and going under. She took off at a run and when she saw the women standing there not making a move to help the girl, she dove into the fast-moving river. Being a strong swimmer, Sage made it to the girl with a few quick strokes. The girl clutched at her. Sage took a deep breath and dove under to get out of the girl's frantic reach and came up underneath her, lifting and pushing her toward shore. Again she dove, and again she pushed until they were both able to touch the sandy bottom.

They waded ashore with Sage holding the girl up. Both were coughing and breathing heavy and the girl collapsed in the grass.

Sage scowled at the stunned women. "Why didn't any of you try to help her?" she demanded.

"We...we...would have drowned too..." Abagail finally said, fighting her tears.

"None of you can swim?" Sage asked. They all shook their heads no.

"Mercy ventured too far, where the water gets deep. We told her not to, but she would not listen," the other young girl whimpered.

"I thank you for saving my daughter's life. You are certainly a blessing to us," Abagail said, looking down. "And I'm fearfully sorry to have swooned when you arrived and caused so much trouble for you."

"You're welcome, Abagail, and what is past is past," Sage said softly, and she turned away without another word spoken.

"That was a foolish thing to do, Sage, brave but foolish," Morgan admonished her. "You could have drowned too, or been hurt, or been stoned for showing so much of your body. You must get dressed, and quickly, before any of the men come!"

Sage understood these were different times and stepped back into her heavy skirt. Although the blouse was still damp, she put that back on too and trudged up the hill away from the river without a word.

Sage put another log in the old wood stove and pulled a chair closer. She finger-combed her short hair to help it dry quicker. She had removed her wet clothes and draped them over a chair near the stove so they would dry. Morgan had given her a long shift to put on, however the air was still cool. The river might have been warm in the shallows, but it was cold in the deeper parts, and she shivered. Morgan handed her a cup of tea.

"You have not said a word since saving that foolish girl," Morgan said, sitting in a chair across from Sage. "May I ask why you did that?"

"I saved her because it was the right thing to do!" Sage said. "I don't understand the people of this time! All of you would have let that girl die and without even *trying* to help her."

"No one here can...swim, my dear. You dove into that water without any hesitation at all, and you moved so quickly to reach her.

The women will be talking about this for quite some time to come," Morgan said. "May I ask how you can to do that?"

"Do what? Swim? My father taught me how when I was very young. It feels as if I've always been able to swim, I don't even think about it anymore. Why?"

"It is unusual, that is all," Morgan observed, thinking what a strange person this Sage was, strange and…nice to have around.

Sage stood and stirred the tomato sauce bubbling on the back of the stove. "I'll need some herbs for the sauce. Will you show me where you grow them?" Sage put her cape around her shoulders and put her bonnet back on before following Morgan outside.

Morgan picked a stem and held it out to Sage who sniffed it.

"Thyme, yes that can be used." They went through the same process, with Sage taking or rejecting various herbs that Morgan offered to her. She chopped and then added them to the sauce.

"I admit that smells very enticing, Sage-from-the-future. Will it be eaten with more of that pasta?"

"Yes. Would you like to learn how to make that? It's really quite easy," Sage smiled.

There came a knock at the door.

"Do you know who is out there?" Sage asked, cautiously.

"I do believe it is Abagail and Mercy," Morgan said calmly and opened the door.

"Miss Sage, I would like to thank you for saving me today," Mercy said with tears in her eyes and a curtsey. "I like being in the water. Could you teach me to…swim like you do?"

"If I'm here long enough, Mercy, yes, I will try to teach you to swim. I do not know when I will need to leave though, so promise me you will be very careful not to go deep into the river."

"Oh, I promise, Miss Sage. Thank you!" she curtsied again and stepped aside to give her mother room.

"I would like to give you this, Miss Sage, as a thank you. My husband died of the pox several years ago; I now have only my daughter. I would have died myself from grief if she had drowned," Abagail handed her a beautiful white bonnet with fine embroidery on the crown.

"Thank you Abagail. It's lovely. It was not necessary to give me anything, but I accept it." Sage smiled at the woman, who curtsied like her daughter had done. They turned away without another word and left.

"I think I've made a friend," Sage said, closing the door.

A friend is nice to have, Morgan thought silently.

"What do you call this?" Morgan asked over dinner.

"Spaghetti."

CHAPTER THIRTY ONE

———————⊛———————

Morgan had piled some winter quilts on the floor near the woodstove for her to make a nest-bed, and Sage slept much better.

The old sorceress woke before her new companion and sat on one of the hard chairs watching the girl sleep. The covers rose and fell with the easy breathing, and Morgan smiled. This girl, this Sage-from-the-future, was such an oddity. It was obvious that she was highly intelligent and had multiple talents, and Morgan wondered if all women were like this in the future. At the same time, some of the most common and simple chores seemed to evade her. Sage had explained it as a difference in culture. When Morgan questioned how drawing water from a well could be different, Sage tried to explain plumbing. When Morgan asked more questions about this plumbing, Sage reminded her of a promise to her future self that she would not ruin the coming years for her past self. It was all so confusing.

Still, Morgan liked this girl, which was odd in itself. Mayhap it was because the girl was not afraid of her, like everyone else. She would have to ponder this more.

Sage turned over and opened her eyes. "Good morning, is it tea yet?" She yawned and sat up, pulling the quilts closer around her.

"Yes, it has brewed while you slept," Morgan handed her a cup of the weak tea.

"So, what is on the agenda for today?" Sage asked, sipping carefully; yesterday, the tea almost scalded her tongue.

"You continue to speak so strangely. Please explain your question; that was a question, was it not?"

"Yes, it was a question," Sage had to think what she had said that was confusing. "Ah, agenda...an agenda is a list of things to do. So, what are we going to do today?"

"I need to take some of my garments to the river and rinse them. I go on a day the other women do not. As you may have noticed, they dislike my presence," she quickly added. "And the water buckets need refilling from the drinking well, and I will tend my plants today as well."

"I can help with all that. What do we do first?"

"It is best to do the washing first as it will take the garments all day to dry," Morgan said, frowning. "Do you not wash your clothes this way?"

"No, I put them in a machine that washes them for me, while I do something else and then into a machine that dries them in a short time. We might as well get started." Sage handed Morgan a biscuit from the day before, and washed her own down with the tea.

Sage carried the bundle of clothes Morgan had set out. "This is a lot to wash at one time. How often do you do this?"

"Every month is enough. Are they too heavy for you?" Morgan asked with a grin.

"Not at all, I was only curious about what you do all day."

They had reached the same spot as before, and Sage dropped the bundle on the beach. She removed her shoes and skirt, and stepped into the warm shallow water. "I'm going a little deeper so I won't get river sand in your clothes; the water is still stirred up from yesterday's rain." She stopped in the thigh deep water and rinsed a piece at a time.

"They will need to hang for a bit to let the water run off else they be too heavy to carry back."

"Hmm…let's wring them out." And she showed Morgan how two people working together could get things done quickly and efficiently.

They draped the still damp clothes on the bushes and branches beside the house to dry in the breeze and sun.

"I'll get water while you tend the garden. Then we need to talk more."

"What is it you wish to talk about?" Morgan questioned. The longer this girl was around the fonder of her she grew. Morgan knew this was not good as the girl might be leaving soon.

"I don't know. I've been here three days now, and I still don't know what it is I'm supposed to do. It wasn't saving the child in the well, or Mercy from the river or I would have gone back already. There still must be something for me to do with…you." Sage picked up the heavy wooden bucket and walked the short distance into town and to the central well.

Sage found Abagail at the well and set her bucket down, while she waited for the other woman to finish.

"Are you well today, Abagail? And how is Mercy?" Sage asked politely.

"We are well, thank you. Because of what you have done for us, I fear I must warn you the other women have not been kind, and Proctor is now watching for you so he can question you about the events of yesterday."

"I am not afraid of him," Sage responded.

"You should be! It is he that sits on the Court of Oyer and Terminer, and he means to do you harm."

"Move aside Abagail," coming up behind her, Proctor unnecessarily pushed the woman out of his way. "Miss Sage Aster, this court wishes to question you about the claim of witchcraft that has been leveled at you."

"Witchcraft? I have done no such thing," Sage stood her ground and pulled up a bucket of water, ignoring the old man.

"I have six witnesses that swear they saw you walk on the river to pull poor Mercy from drowning in the deep water! Did you also bewitch her into the river and then save her to glorify yourself?"

"I did not walk on the water, good sir, I swam under the water to save that girl's life," Sage corrected him and poured the water into her bucket.

"Then you admit it!" he said triumphantly.

"I admit nothing. If that were true, then throw me back into the deep part of the river and see if I can come back out," Sage challenged.

"That could be arranged," he said slyly.

"Oh yeah, throw me into the briar patch, you fat, pompous, old fart!" Angry, Sage picked up the half-filled bucket and turned away. Proctor grabbed her arm and she swung the bucket at his head striking him soundly, then she bolted.

Thoroughly frightened over the situation, she ran in between two of the buildings, sliding on the dew slick cobblestones, dodging everyone in her way. Her heart was pounding harder than she thought possible, and she tried to catch her breath, knowing she had to get to Morgan. Morgan was the only one who could save her. One of Proctor's minions snuck up on her as she leaned against the building planning her escape, and he clamped his big hand around her thin wrist. She struggled and couldn't get loose as he dragged her away. As a last resort, she leaned down and bit his hand as hard as she could. He screamed and let her go.

Sage started running again, ducking behind buildings and trees. She watched the shadows on the ground and was warned when another was coming around the corner, giving her enough time to hide again. Adrenalin was pumping through her so hard it was making her dizzy. She was so scared she got turned around and was actually running further away from Morgan and safety. Seeing an opportunity, she picked up her long skirts and ran through the center of town and into the woods.

The fear Sage felt was driving her deeper into the forest. She knew she needed to stop and get her bearings. Right, she needed to go right and back to the road. She could see a dozen people chasing her now, and she fled once more, her legs tangling in her long skirt slowing her down. Her heart hammered in her chest, threatening to explode, and she almost fainted when a big burly man came at her with a deadly looking pitchfork.

"Morgan!" she screamed and tripped as her long cloak caught on a low hanging branch.

Morgan lifted her head from the task of weeding the flowers when she heard the girl scream her name. She spread her senses out to find Sage and took off at a run in that direction. When she saw the big man poised over a cowering Sage with the pitchfork and the others closing in on her, she yelled "NO!" and sent a massive wave of blue energy out from her hands, knocking everyone to the ground, unconscious.

She helped the shaking and winded Sage to stand.

"I knew you would save me, Morgan," Sage sobbed.

"I could not let them harm you, my Sage-from-the-future," Morgan wept, holding the trembling girl.

"I know." And Sage vanished leaving behind only her new bonnet.

CHAPTER THIRTY TWO

K nowing Sage always returned within a few minutes of departing, Morgan stayed in the massive chamber to wait for her.

Sage appeared a minute later, crumpled to the floor, twigs and leaves tangled in her short dark hair. Morgan's energy was fading a bit more every day, and she pulled on every last bit of her strength to take Sage upstairs to her room, and then sat on the edge of the bed while she combed Sage's short hair free of the four-hundred-year-old debris. "Sleep, my Sage-from-the-future," she said softly and settled in the padded chair beside the bed to rest.

───────◉───────

"I do believe Morgan is upstairs with Miss Sage," Henry told Lyle. "Quite honestly, I'm a bit concerned," he whispered. "She's been up there for two days. I've taken her a tray twice a day, but she's eating very little."

"I'll go up and try to coax her down," Lyle said, feeling the butler's concern.

"Thank you, sir. I'll see to making Jon and your guest comfortable."

"Morgan?" Lyle said, opening the door to Sage's room wider. "May I come in?"

"Oh yes, dear. Of course, you can," Morgan stood and stretched. "She's still sleeping after her last...trip, although she should wake soon."

"Where was she this time?" Lyle crossed the large room silently. His footfalls muffled by the plush carpeting.

"She was with me, in Salem, 1692. I think meeting me as I was back then was traumatic for her," Morgan yawned.

"Well, if she's back, then it was successful, yes?"

"Indeed it was, *and* she came back with all her own clothes," Morgan chuckled.

"Come downstairs and have some lunch with us. You know she will wake when she's ready," Lyle suggested. "Oh, and we brought a guest with us." He reached out and stroked Paw's furry head. The cat had followed him up the stairs and quickly took his place on Sage's bed.

Morgan clutched Lyle's arm as they descended the long sweeping staircase, and still leaning heavily on his arm and her staff, they headed for the sun-room.

"Elem?" Morgan stopped suddenly. "Why is he here?" her voice raised in pitch. She wasn't pleased to see him at all.

"We think you should hear him out, Morgan. Perhaps, he can help Sage." Lyle seated Morgan at the head of the table.

"Is something wrong with Sage?" Elem rose quickly to his feet, dread lacing his deep voice.

"She's sleeping," Morgan said sternly, settling into her usual chair. Henry was quickly at her side with a bowl of rich New England clam chowder. "Thank you, Henry. I'm sorry you've been so worried about me. I promise I won't skip any more meals." She turned to their guest. "Now, what do you have to tell me that is so important you had to come all the way here from your cruise ship?"

"Morgan, please give him a chance," Jon pleaded against Morgan's rude attitude.

Elem sat back down and looked long at Morgan. "I'm remembering snippets of another life, and they involve Sage. I know I've never met her before, but I swear I have. It's difficult to explain." He looked down at his age-spotted hands.

"We think he's Ethan!" Jon said.

"And Edward," Lyle finished.

Morgan set her spoon down and looked at Elem—really looked at him. She saw the faintest shimmer of blue and gold around him, an energy only she could see. "I see, and what do you propose to do about it?"

"I don't know. I think that's up to Sage. Can I see her?" Elem stared at Morgan, tilting his head to one side, confused at how he felt she too was familiar to him. She also wore a blue crystal similar to the one that Sage always wore.

Morgan closed her eyes in thought and stretched out her senses. "She should be down shortly. I believe she's in the shower now. Jon, be a dear, and ask Henry to prepare Sage a hearty breakfast, and to bring her a cup of that chowder first; it was quite good."

Sage stood under the hot shower for what felt like a long time. Her last bath had been in the cold river, and she could still feel the chill in her bones and smelled the wildness on her skin. After toweling off, she brushed her teeth and stared at her image in the mirror. When did she start to look so sad?

She picked over the clothes in her closet and pulled on a pair of soft tan slacks and a deep V-necked copper-colored knit shirt. Her eyes fell on the blue silk dress and she caressed the softness. A random tear fell and slid down her cheek. She brushed it away, took a deep breath and headed down the stairs looking for food.

Sage saw Morgan and the guys sitting in the sun room, her appearance temporarily escaped them. She checked the side board only to find it empty, so she quietly slipped into the kitchen.

Elem felt her presence and looked up, but she wasn't there.

"Ah Miss Sage, I'm happy to see you well again. I will bring you a cup of chowder first, per Miss Morgan, followed by one of Alyce's special breakfasts," Henry said. "They are waiting for you in the sun room."

Sage nodded, afraid to speak yet. Too many emotions were coursing through her. As she pushed open the swinging door to the kitchen, they all looked up and stood. She didn't see him at first, although she could feel him, and she stopped.

Elem stepped from behind Lyle and smiled at her, opening his arms. Tears of joy mixed with surprise ran down her face as she hurried to his embrace. His arms closed around her and held her tight. They stood like that for several long moments, until Jon cleared his throat.

Sage touched Elem's face and caressed his cheek, then reached up and tenderly kissed him. "You don't know how happy I am to see you," she said, wiping the tears away.

"Sit and eat, Sage, you must be famished. You've been asleep for three days this time," Morgan said, her eyes flicking to Elem.

Henry arrived with the soup, and Sage's hands shook when she picked up the spoon. When she was finished, he removed the bowl and set a platter in front of her with all her favorites.

"Why was she asleep for three days?" Elem asked Morgan, pulling his chair closer to Sage.

"We can discuss that after she's eaten." Morgan picked up the sandwich Henry had brought for her and took a bite, washing it down with coffee. "Henry will bring you anything you want if you're hungry."

"We already ate, Morgan, but thank you," Lyle and Jon left to walk in the gardens while the three worked things out.

———————————————•❁•———————————————

Sage pushed away her mostly eaten food; she had devoured the crispy hash browns and all of the bacon first. A piece of cinnamon toast still in her hand, she smiled at Elem, and then turned to Morgan.

"I was there for four days, but you know that right?"

"Yes, I do," Morgan smiled sadly.

"You remember me from then?"

"I do. It's very strange having two sets of memories, the then and the now. The new memories are quickly taking over, my-Sage-from-the-future," Morgan said with a sad smile.

Sage inhaled quickly at the familiar endearment. "Did I help?"

"Very much."

"I still don't understand what my mission was."

"It was to bring me your friendship," Morgan answered with tightness in her chest.

"I see. What happened after I left?"

"Much washed over me in a short period of time with your departure. I left the villagers that were attacking you in the forest while I went into town to retrieve a horse and small wagon. While there, I removed the spell from everyone and everything. Their gardens grew well after that," Morgan smiled, remembering that was a concern of Sage's. "I took what few things I valued, packed them into the wagon and left to find another place to settle. As I reached the crest of the hill, I looked back at the woods and set those people to rights. They remembered nothing but a sudden surge in wild flowers. My garden however, turned to twigs and dust. Oh, I found your baseball cap and later burned it so it would not be found although I will say I was tempted to keep such a strange looking thing."

Sage nodded.

"I don't understand what you two are discussing," Elem protested. "Sage from the future? Are you from another time?"

"No, this is my time. Morgan has sent me to the past to right some wrongs."

"There is yet another wrong to right," Morgan stood. "Please come with me—both of you."

Hand in hand, Elem and Sage followed Morgan into her chambers; a wave of her hand materialized the hidden door into the cavernous magic room.

"Even this looks familiar," Elem said.

"It should. I fashioned it after Haedre's room," Morgan turned to him, "where we grew up, Evon." She touched his forehead and dragging her finger gently down between his eyes, releasing him from the spell she had placed on him over seven hundred years earlier.

He gasped, fighting for breath. A clarity blossomed in his eyes, turning Elem's brown eyes to the bright blue that belonged to Evon and then back again.

"Morgan, my sister. I have missed you." Evon/Elem said.

"Evon, I'm so sorry for what I did to you. Will you please forgive me?" Morgan said shedding the tears she had held inside for almost eight-hundred years.

"Of course, I forgive you. You're my sister, and I love you," Evon/Elem embraced the weeping Morgan.

Morgan felt the weight of ages lift from her; her heart widened, and she felt love, real love, for the first time in her long life.

Sage had stood off to the side, watching the reunion. She smiled seeing such deep emotion coming from Morgan. She felt a tingle from the blue crystal still hanging around her neck and as Elem watched in shock, Sage disappeared.

———◆———

It was cold and getting dark. Sage shivered as the heavily falling snow coated her thin shirt. There was a bright light coming from a fire on the other side of whatever it was she was standing near. Letting her eyes roam the coming darkness, she could see a large wheel beside her and following the lines, she saw the covered wagon, several of them forming a circle. The year would be late 1700's, perhaps early 1800's.

What am I doing here, Morgan? She thought silently.

There came the pounding of horse hooves and the wild whooping yells of the riders. Those inside the circle started their own shouting as defensive positions were taken. Sage stood frozen in wonderment outside the protection of the wagons. When she saw the first Indian ride into view, painted with white, black, and yellow slashes on his face, she stared in fear and clutched at the necklace. The rider drew his bow back and shot an arrow straight at her.

"Get me out of here!" she cried. The arrow sliced through her fading image.

———◆———

"What happened to Sage? She just vanished. Where did she go?" an alarmed Elem yelled at Morgan.

"I...I don't know! I didn't send her anywhere this time. She can send herself home anytime, but she can't leave by herself....I don't think," Morgan approached the magic circle in time to see an arrow drop where Sage had been. Within two seconds, Sage appeared too, unconscious and barely breathing.

"Put her on the bed!" Morgan directed. Elem easily picked

her up and carried her to the other room, laying her on Morgan's small bed.

Morgan hovered over Sage, searching with her eyes that could see what others couldn't.

"Her aura is ruptured, likely from being shot with that arrow at the same moment she time shifted."

"Can you fix it? I haven't used my magic for hundreds of years, Morgan. I don't know what to do." Evon/Elem sat beside Sage and took her hand.

"That's a good start, Evon. She loves you; it could be what she needs right now to pull through." She looked closely at the man who loved her Sage, loved her as much as she did, and she knew what needed to be done. She removed the star stone from around Sage's neck.

"Evon, this stone is yours, it's the one I took from you so very long ago, and it should help return your powers to you." She placed the enchanted serpent around his neck and watched his eyes turn blue again and stay that color. She then took her own stone and placed it around Sage's neck. "Draw on Evon's power, but you must remain Elem as that is who she knows and loves. We will need to create a trinity between the stones. Stay on the other side of her and continue to hold her hand."

Morgan grasped her staff and tapped it on the floor at the foot of the bed. It stood and glowed blue. The air cracked with blue light, going from the staff to Evon, to Sage, to the staff again with Morgan in the center. Morgan sat on the vacated chair, placing her right hand on Sage's forehead and the left on her abdomen. "We've come full circle, my Sage," and Morgan began to glow. A mist of blue and white energy poured from her: blue for her power, white for her love, and as the mist settled onto and into Sage, it left Morgan. She slumped, having sacrificed herself for the one person she loved; the one person who loved *her* for herself: Sage.

———•✦•———

Lyle grabbed Jon's arm. "Morgan needs us!" and they ran to her chambers. Without knocking, Lyle opened the door slowly, and they stood there as witnesses to the miracle happening. When Morgan collapsed, they stepped forward.

CHAPTER THIRTY THREE

———————•—❋—•———————

S age opened her eyes and blinked several times. She looked up and saw Elem and she smiled, yet saw sadness in his eyes. After a deep breath, she turned her head and saw Morgan's body. At first, she was confused, but when she saw Lyle and Jon a few feet away weeping, she knew Morgan was dead and closed her eyes again.

"Help me up," she reached out for Elem. Though her legs were wobbly, she went to Lyle and Jon, giving each a hug. "I'm glad you were here to see this, guys. I would not have believed what just happened if others hadn't seen it too."

"What did happen, Sage?" Jon asked, wiping his tears away.

"I spontaneously traveled back in time…no, not spontaneously, the crystal sent me back. Morgan told me the crystal's power was getting stronger, she didn't know how or why though; I think it was a combination due to the presence of Evon and Elem's memory returning. Anyway, it was winter and snowing, and I was on the outside of a circle of covered wagons that was being attacked by Indians. I begged the crystal to send me home, and as I shifted, an Indian shot me with his arrow."

"Morgan said the arrow ruptured your aura," Elem added. "You were dying."

"And she gave her life for mine? Why?" Sage whimpered, tears now running down her cheeks.

"Because she loved you," Elem said. "For nearly eight hundred years she was incapable of love because of the spell she put on me. *You* changed that. You loved her first, here and then back in Salem," he smiled at her, "And then your love for me brought me here, so she could release that spell. When she did that, all those emotions were overwhelming to her." He took a deep breath. "The stones are very powerful, and she had abused them. *They* sent you back, intentionally in harm's way, to test Morgan's new worthiness...and she didn't let us, or them, down. She sacrificed herself for you."

Elem looked deep into her eyes and grinned. "She left you a gift, didn't she?"

Sage smiled when she realized what he meant. "Yes, she did. She is part of me now. I don't have her memories, other than some fondness I will have to think about, but...I have her knowledge and her powers."

Elem lifted Morgan's lifeless body, and placed it gently on the bed in a final repose. With him and Sage on one side, and Lyle and Jon on the other, they joined hands and wept for the loss of their dear friend. After a few minutes, they all stepped back.

"I know Morgan will understand this," Sage drew on her new powers and passed her hands over Morgan, aging her.

"Why did you do that?" Jon questioned with a sniffle.

"Because, dearest, this is still the 21st century, and there will be questions over Morgan's death...unless she died of old age," Lyle explained, a hitch in his sad voice.

"Would you please call Henry and Alyce in here? We have some explaining to do before calling the authorities," Sage said, wondering what she would say to Morgan's long time and faithful servants.

"Oh, poor Miss Morgan," Alyce cried, reaching out to touch the hand that was growing cold.

"You don't seem surprised that…she looks old," Sage questioned.

"Miss Sage," Henry interrupted, "Alyce and I have known Morgan for a very long time. And for most of that time we've known about her…uniqueness. I've been watching her grow weaker and weaker for two or three years now, and she did confide in me that she was dying. Understand, she was okay with that, but she also wanted to make amends. For what, I don't know." Henry looked long at Morgan's still body. "May I ask how…?"

"She gave her life to save Sage," Elem offered. "And since you've known about Morgan's powers, you should know that Sage now has them."

"How delightful!" Henry exclaimed softly. "I'm happy that her legacy will live on."

"There were times when I was afraid of Morgan's powers. Now that they are mine, I understand them. I know not only how to use them, but also why and when. It's really a wonderful and comforting feeling," Sage confessed to Elem. "I hope I do justice to her faith in me."

CHAPTER THIRTY FOUR

———•—✦—•———

"I hope you will forgive the intrusion, and no disrespect intended, but I do need to speak with the house staff—privately," the officer had said after having taken down all the basic information from those four.

"Of course," Sage replied. "Make yourself comfortable, and I'll send for them. We'll wait in the library for you." She looked at Lyle and nodding, he went to the kitchen to bring Alyce and Henry out to the greeting room.

The coroner's wagon pulled out from under the portico, leaving behind six distraught people. The doctor and the police officer had been polite and understanding as they questioned the four friends and two servants.

"I am deeply sorry for your loss. I'll be in touch if there is anything further I need," the officer said before he left.

———•—✦—•———

Sage, Elem, Jon, and Lyle gathered around the small table that Sage and Morgan had so often shared their meal at.

"What's next?" Jon asked.

"We need to plan some kind of memorial gathering for her," Sage gave a rueful laugh. "Although I think it will be attended by only the six of us. Morgan didn't have any friends besides us, that I know of, and I understand her beliefs didn't fall within conventional lines. Since she was eight-hundred-years old, I assumed she would live forever, so I never thought to ask her about funeral arrangements or burial."

"We talked about that very thing when we were young," Elem said. "Cremation was our first choice and no preference on what to do with the ashes."

"I think one of her antique vases would be appropriate," Sage said. She looked at her two close friends. "You two knew her longer than I did, so you should pick one out."

The four were still in the library hours later when Henry interrupted them.

"Excuse me, there is someone here to see you," he said, handing Sage a business card, "Miss Morgan's attorney, Floyd Astrape. Shall I show him in?"

"Attorney? Of course, perhaps he can help us with some of the details," Sage said.

"Mr. Astrape, welcome. Did Morgan have an appointment with you today?" Elem asked.

"No, sir. I heard the call on my police scanner. Please accept my deepest condolences. Mrs. Alsteen was a wonderful and remarkable lady," the attorney said. "As part of her recent changes to her will, she asked that her estate be settled quickly. I understand this is a difficult time, but these were her wishes." He pulled some papers out of his briefcase and scanned them, though he knew them by heart. He read off the beneficiaries' names.

"We are all here, Mr. Astrape. Is this something we can deal with now? It's been a very disturbing day for all of us," Sage said, another tear trickling down her cheek.

"Even though the estate is large, the will is short, so yes." After

Henry and Alyce joined them, he read the terms and the bequests and finally said, "And you, Miss Sage Aster, are to receive everything else, which is quite substantial. It will take a few weeks to disperse the funds; however, the abundant cash in the checking account is at your immediate disposal."

Lyle, Jon, Henry, and Alyce were stunned at the amount of their bequests.

Sage only nodded. "I guess I won't have to move then. Would you care for a drink, Mr. Astrape? We were about to raise a glass to Morgan. We miss her very much already." She said with a hitch in her voice.

The serpent around her neck purred. "We have one more thing to do, here and now, don't we?" she asked Elem.

"Yes, my Sage." He turned to Lyle and Jon. "Please come with us to the magic room. We would like you to bear witness."

Elem removed his necklace and put the serpent on the altar. Sage did the same. The two enchanted serpents slithered in ecstasy to finally be together, and wound around each other. They gave one last look at Elem and Sage, their masters, and with their heads pressed together in an embrace, they turned to stone—together forever. Then they turned to ash, leaving behind two perfect gold eggs.

Elem faced Sage, his crystal set on his open palm. "Sage, I give to you my heart, and my love, for all eternity."

"Elem, I give to you my heart, and my love, for all eternity," Sage repeated. They then pressed their crystal to the other's heart. The stones glowed bright blue and their bodies absorbed it into their hearts, never to be lost again.

Elem smiled down at her, "And as my bonding gift to you," he said and closed his eyes. His features began to shift: his gray hair turned blond, the wrinkles that etched deep in his face disappeared, and loose skin tightened. He was thirty years old again.

"That wasn't necessary. I loved you just the way you were," she said.

"I know, but as we go through this life together, I'll not have others questioning why a beautiful young woman is with a tired old man."

Lyle and Jon gasped at the transformation.

"What are you going to do with those eggs?" Jon asked.

"I'm not sure of their purpose yet. It will come to me when the time is right," Sage said.

CHAPTER THIRTY FIVE

———•✦•———

T wo weeks later the four friends were sitting in the sun room waiting for Henry to bring their lunch. In spite of the large endowment each of them had been given, both Henry and Alyce stayed on in their same positions as cherished household servants. Their only comment was they had nowhere else to go, and they had been with Morgan for so long, that the big house was their home.

"Oh, yum," Sage exclaimed, "a lightly toasted Reuben sandwich. Who wants half?"

Henry leaned down to whisper, "Miss Sage, if you give half of that away, Alyce will be offended! She made it just for you."

He placed everyone's sandwich in front of them, and then set a tureen of homemade beef barley soup in the center with four cups and then disappeared from the room.

"Have you two decided yet when you're moving in here?" Elem asked. The move had been discussed in depth, however the actual date had not been settled on.

"We thought we would give the two of you a few more weeks alone before descending upon you and ruining your honeymoon," Jon snickered. "Besides, our lease doesn't expire for another month."

"Well, you need to decide which suite you want. We've got a contractor coming this afternoon to discuss the renovations," Elem said, taking a bite of his salami and Swiss on pumpernickel.

"What are you having done?" Lyle was immediately interested.

"We really want an addition: a ballroom off the greeting room, so we can dance and an apartment suite on the upper level for us. Of course, it will mean losing this room or relocating it. I'd also like to see more of the plumbing upgraded," Sage explained. "And with six of us in the house, Alyce will need a bigger and more modern kitchen."

"Why not convert that huge room off Morgan's chambers into a ballroom? That's probably what it was originally," Lyle said.

Elem and Sage looked at him in astonishment. "I think we still need that room, dear. However, I'd like to turn her sleeping chamber into a study, and that's where you come in, Jon. I want it lively and colorful, bright and inviting."

Jon beamed.

"And what do you propose we use the magic room for?" Elem asked Sage later.

"Ah, magic?" Sage said with a grin. "Think of all the good things we can do with our new powers. Besides, I want to take one more trip to the past." With the gift of Morgan's powers, Sage also received a calmness and a maturity beyond her actual years.

Elem was rightfully alarmed. "And where, or rather when, do you want to go? I certainly don't like how your last trip ended."

"I want to give Helen back her ruby necklace," Sage said. "In 1930, before she meets Morgan. There's no danger, and I certainly can't lose my star stone." She touched her chest, and her skin glowed a faint hue of blue.

"Why are you giving it back? She obviously wanted you to have it."

"I believe I was meant to wear the necklace to help you remember who you were, and now that you know, it has served its purpose. I think Helen should have it back," Sage explained.

Elem smiled down at her. "Your thoughtfulness is just one of the many reasons I love you." He kissed her lightly. "So, when will you go and what can I do?"

"I think right now would be good. I don't want this on my mind and cloud my judgement when we discuss things with the contractor."

———————— ❖ ————————

Sage dressed in the same slacks, green sweater, and jacket she wore on the *Titanic*, hoping it would help trigger Helen's memory. She looked one last time at the ruby and diamond necklace.

"It's beautiful," Elem said.

"Yes, it is," Sage replied closing the velvet lined jeweler's box and slipping it into her pocket. "I've never asked you, but Helen might want to know: what happened to Ethan? Morgan said he went back to England in 1932 to settle their father's estate, and they never heard from him again."

"Six months after he arrived back in England, Ethan fell off his horse playing polo and broke his neck. His death was instant." Elem frowned, tapping into the old memories. "I'll have you know I'm having a difficult time with the he—I thing…I am him, but he was never me."

"Sweetheart, you have Evon's goodness, Edward's compassion, and Ethan's loyalty, plus his love of dancing. All of that makes you, you, and I love all of the "you's," so don't fret about it. I have something I need to do first, I'll be right back." When she returned, Sage stood in the circle. "You need to draw the circles of fire, and I will do the rest." Sage found she was quickly adapting to having Morgan's power.

Elem walked around her, drawing the lines with the staff and, facing her, drew the last one and she disappeared.

Sage reappeared at the front door of the big house, as she knew she would, and knocked. Helen looked shocked when she answered the door.

"Hello, Helen. Do you remember me? May I come in?" Sage said smiling.

"Of course, I remember you! Sage Astor!" Helen blurted out. "Yes, please come in."

"I won't take much of your time, Helen," Sage said. "I wanted to see you again, see how you're doing, and to return this to you." She pulled the jewelers box out of her pocket and handed it to Helen.

Helen opened the box and gasped. "But I wanted you to have it, Sage, as a thank you. I didn't realize how big of a thank you that would be at the time; please keep it." She held it out to Sage who stepped around the gesture.

"Can we sit and talk for a few minutes? There are a few things you should know."

They settled on an ornate settee in the greeting room, Helen putting the box between them.

"We owe you Ethan's life. If you hadn't pushed him over the railing he would have drowned like so many others...like we thought you did," the older woman frowned.

"I'm pleased he survived. What I told you back then about time travel was true. I was from the future; I'm still from the future, Helen. I won't even be born for another sixty-some years. The year is 2021, and I'm twenty-six years old—still. To me, it's only been seven months since I met you on the *Titanic*."

"This is a bit much to take in, however, I believe you. You

haven't aged a bit in the eighteen years it's been for me. Although, you do *seem* older and much more mature and confident."

"I've been through a great deal in the last several months, and I think it has aged me—on the inside at least," Sage smiled slowly.

"Oh, Ethan will be so happy to see you! He's checking on a tenant and will be back in an hour or so."

"That wouldn't be a good idea. I can't stay, and if he sees me, my leaving will only hurt him again," she explained.

Helen frowned again. "I will try to understand. He's been a good brother, and I don't want him distressed."

Sage looked around and smiled. "I see you've done well for yourself."

"Yes, we have. I must tell you, you were very right about that Humphrey Tuttle and about the stock market. I tried to follow what you told me that night." She paused in thought. "Why won't you keep the necklace?"

"It has served its purpose for me, is all I can tell you, and I'm very grateful for that," Sage said, standing.

"Sage, I haven't met the person you told me to look for, not yet."

"I know, it will be soon though, so don't give up your walks in the park," Sage smiled. "Oh, I have something else for you," she pulled out three sealed envelopes from her pocket. "This one is for you to open any time. I might be pushing the time stream a bit, but it's a list of companies for you to consider investing in." she handed Helen the first envelope. "Please keep these next two safe. This one is to ease your mind; don't open until this date in 1933. This next one is for the woman you will meet. Give it to her in 1950." Sage knew that in 1933, after Ethan left and never returned, having died, Helen would be comforted by knowing he died quickly, reincarnated, and they were together again.

Helen read the envelope, *"Go with the flow.* That's what you told me to do."

"In time, she will understand what it means." Sage stood. "Can I look around some? I'd like to see how the house was originally."

"Originally?"

"Oh, I live here now in 2021, and I'm looking into some renovations. May I?" Sage walked down the hall toward the library and passed the door that would eventually lead to Morgan's chambers. She stopped and opened the heavy wooden door. Behind the door was a closet. She continued to the library and saw it was much like it would be in ninety years.

"Have you found the hidden safe yet?" Helen asked.

"A hidden safe? No I haven't. Is it in here?"

Helen pushed on a panel next to the fireplace and exposed a large safe. She dialed the combination, and put the envelopes and the necklace box inside. "The combination is Ethan's birthdate," she giggled like she did on the *Titanic,* and it warmed Sage's heart.

"I need to go, Helen." Sage gave the woman a long hug. "And so you do know this is all true…." Sage placed her hand over her heart; the crystal inside glowed and she disappeared.

───────── ✳ ─────────

Sage reappeared inside the magic circle and saw Elem starting to sit in a chair.

"Is everything alright?" he asked. "You were gone only a second!"

"Everything is perfect, my love. Come with me, we have something to check out." Sage led him to the library, where she pressed on the panel beside the fireplace and exposed the safe.

"How did you…?"

"Helen showed it to me. Now, you need to tap into Ethan's memories again. What was his birthdate?" she asked.

"That's easy, it's June 21, 1888. Edward's was June 21, 1828. Mine is June 21, 1948," he replied. "And Evon's was June 21, 1221."

"Interesting, mine is June 21, 1995. We were all born on the summer solstice. The date must be one the connections that drew us together," Sage said, dialing the numbers. The safe clicked and opened. The envelopes were gone, as Sage had hoped they would be. In their place, were several jewelry boxes. She opened the first one and saw the ruby and diamond necklace, and she laughed. "Helen was determined I would get these."

She handed another box to Elem. Opening it, they saw the emerald and diamond necklace that Helen had worn to dinner the night the *Titanic* sank.

"I remember this one. It was Helen's other favorite," Elem said. "There's a note." He handed it to Sage.

"My deepest thank you for letting me know about Ethan, and that you two are finally together. Morgan has no interest in my jewels, so they are now yours to do with as you wish. Wear them at least once. Love, Helen."

"You told her?"

"I had to. Morgan said she was saddened the rest of her life not knowing what happened to her beloved Ethan. It was to give her peace, and we should all have peace in our lives."

They opened the others and found a diamond choker necklace, and a sapphire necklace with a matching bracelet.

"Their mother had good taste and she loved sparkly things," Elem laughed, and put the boxed jewels back in the safe.

"Do you know what tomorrow is?" Elem asked after dinner. They were having coffee in front of the fireplace, having finished a scrumptious ribeye steak with Alyce's secret sauce.

"Tomorrow? I'm sorry, Elem, I lose track of...time when I time travel," Sage apologized.

"It's June 21, *our* birthday. I say we go out on the town with Lyle and Jon," he said.

203

"You've grown quite fond of them, haven't you?" she smiled knowingly.

"Yes, I have. They've taken such good care of you, and Morgan, and they're fun, and funny, and all around nice guys. What's not to like?"

"We'll call them in the morning. Tonight, though, belongs to us," Sage kissed him lovingly.

CHAPTER THIRTY SIX

———————◦❋◦———————

"So, what did the contractor have to say yesterday?" Lyle asked over coffee.

"It was a most enlightening two hours," Sage admitted. "We have a room I didn't know existed!"

"A hidden room? How exciting," Jon said.

"Not hidden, just not obvious," Elem replied. "This house is so large we really haven't had time to explore all of it, and since it's so big there might be more."

"Let's not get ahead of ourselves, dear," Sage said to Elem. "It's more interesting if they hear how it unfolded." She sipped her orange juice and continued. "We told the contractor, Will Singleton, what we wanted to end up with. He then took time to walk completely around the house outside, looked at where we wanted the addition located, the green houses, all of it."

"Knowing we could erase his memory if we needed to, we then let him wander the house—lower level only."

"Even the magic room?" Jon asked in surprise.

"Even the magic room," she said. "I had been thinking about what you said concerning that room having been a ballroom and let him see it. By the way, it was never a ballroom. When I visited Helen in 1930 the room didn't exist, and Morgan's chamber was a closet! Morgan must have done the remodeling and added it later.

"Anyway," Elem continued, "Will walked around the room, nodding his head and writing notes in a little book. He looked behind the tapestries and found windows we didn't know were there. Windows were a concern of ours since we want lots of light in the house. He even jumped up and down a couple of times testing the solidness of the floor." Elem laughed at the memory.

"When he suggested tearing out the altar, calling it a built-in desk, and we told him absolutely not, he said a cabinet would suffice to hide it and by making it a large cabinet, we could house the sound system in it too," Sage went on. "Then he asked about the room on the other side of the east wall, and if we wanted to add that to the ballroom. He has the most amazing eye for spatial anomaly."

"What room on the east wall?" Lyle questioned.

"Come, we'll show you!" Sage took them down the hall past the library. There was a large double door that blended in so well with the dark paneling it was almost invisible. Elem opened the left door easily, the right door having the astragal secured to the floor. He reached down and pulled the pin, opening the second door wide.

"Wow..." Jon breathed, stepping into the huge room.

"Yeah, pretty impressive, isn't it?" Sage giggled, "And all this time we never knew it was here. Will spotted it from outside."

"What are you going to do with it?" Lyle asked.

"Will suggested turning it into the master suite, sectioning it off into a sitting room with a fireplace that backs up to the fireplace in the library, and a bedroom with a walk-in closet and bath," Elem said. "I rather like the idea."

"So do I," Sage smiled. "And by remodeling the magic room only slightly, we won't have to make any exterior changes."

"When does he start?" Jon asked excitedly.

"Next week, and that will give *you* some time to work on the magic room," Sage said.

"What is it you want me to do?" Jon questioned.

"All those tapestries need to come down, carefully, and then stored. That will be the first thing. Come on let's go back to the other room."

Jon looked behind each hanging rug and made notes. "Tell me what you envision."

Sage and Elem pointed and walked, describing their ideas.

"Lyle," Jon turned to his partner, "To hell with our lease. We need to move here sooner. I've got at least a year's work to do."

"Six months, Jon. I want to be done by the winter solstice," Sage stated solemnly, "So we can honor what would have been Morgan's eight-hundredth birthday."

"How ironic you two share a birthday," Jon said, when they returned later for the evening out.

"I think it was pre-ordained," Lyle commented, "And I have a present for you Sage, from Morgan."

"From Morgan? How...."

"When you and her left Key West early, she sent me shopping—for this," he handed her a small box.

"Oh. My." Sage gasped. Inside the box was the Atocha ring she had admired weeks earlier.

"It goes perfect with your new necklace, dear," Elem put the emerald and diamond necklace on her and kissed the back of her neck, adding an enchantment that secured the jewels.

"Now, let's go have some fun!" Sage said, slipping on the ring.

They dined at one of the many five-star restaurants in Manhattan, ordering from the tasting menu to sample the table-side grilled lobster, seared sea scallops, smoked trout and ending with Crème Brule. The sommelier brought them a new bottle of wine with each course.

"That was incredible!" Elem said. "Even as good as the food on the cruise ships is maybe this was better. Where to now, Sage?"

"It's your birthday, too. What do you want to do?" she answered.

"Let's go dancing!" he replied with a devilish grin.

Jon and Lyle showed up early the next afternoon toting three suitcases each, plus several boxes. When Sage looked surprised, Jon said, "Well, you told us to move in!"

After unpacking their clothes in one of the suites upstairs and down the hall from the main staircase, they joined Sage and Elem in the magic room.

"In what order are you having the work done?" Jon questioned.

"Actually, we're paying extra for the work to be done simultaneously. Like I said, I want to be done quickly. I've also promised the contractor healthy bonuses for every week early things are completed," Sage said.

"Money is always a good motivator," Elem grinned. "The new ballroom is more a decorating project than construction, although they will be adding an extra bathroom and a wet bar—minor compared to the new bedroom. Are you two ready to start? I want to see how much light is added once we take the tapestries down."

Two hours later, all the tapestries were removed, rolled up, and pushed off to the side of the large room, exposing four huge multi-paned windows, two each on the two outside walls.

"What are we going to do with those?" Lyle asked, pointing to the wall hangings.

"I think for now we should put them in one of the spare rooms upstairs, so they're out of the way of getting damaged," Sage said.

"I've asked Will to come by, so we can all go over selections of materials. I think in the meantime we should also empty Morgan's room."

———————— ✳ ————————

With all the furniture loaded into a moving van for donation to a homeless shelter, Jon paced the empty room deep in thought.

"Does he always do that?" Will Singleton asked.

"Yes," Lyle answered, "And whatever he comes up with will be phenomenal."

"Will, how soon can you get started on the suite?" Elem asked.

"That's one of the things I wanted to discuss today. Would tomorrow be okay to start bringing in tools and materials? I'd like to get the studs in quickly to get your approval on the layout," he answered. "Once done, I'll get in the electricians to run the wiring and the plumber to do the black pipe and rough pipe. I'm personally going to build the new cabinet in the big room. That desk looks really old and as much as I trust my crew, I want that out of sight before they start on the bar."

———————— ✳ ————————

Work went quickly and smoothly. Two months later, Will brought in the painters to complete the new interior walls in the bedroom suite.

"Will, I am truly impressed not only with your work, but with the speed of getting things done," Sage said. The five sat at one of the small bistro tables Jon had selected for the new dance room.

"The crew is sharing in the bonus, ma'am, so they were motivated, and working ten hours a day, six days a week, was plenty of time to do what needed doing," he laughed. "Besides, this was a relatively easy job, and you were easy to work with. You'd be surprised at the grief I get from some of my clients."

Elem brought out a bottle of champagne from behind the new bar and poured five crystal cut flutes. Sage handed Will a check, and he put it in his pocket after folding it.

"Aren't you going to look at it?" she asked.

"Nope, I do have a question though. Why such a big room just to dance?"

Sage smiled at Elem, who grinned and picked up a remote, turning on the new sound system. A tune suitable for waltzing surrounded them. Elem took Sage's hand and led her to the dance floor. Five minutes later the tune ended.

Will sat stunned. "Forget I asked such a dumb question."

"We'll be hosting a small dinner party in a week or two, and we would be delighted if you and your wife could join us," Sage said.

"Thank you. By the way, when do you want me to start on the kitchen?" Will asked.

"As soon as you can."

CHAPTER THIRTY SEVEN

"**W**hat would you like to do this week?" Sage asked Elem over their morning coffee.

"I don't know. I've always had to work for a living, so I've never had this kind of leisure time before—in this life, that is."

"Would you like to see New York? Or maybe some museums?" she suggested.

"Come to think of it, one thing I've always regretted not taking the time to see was the Smithsonian. Have you ever been there?" he asked.

Sage grinned.

She booked them into the same hotel Morgan had chosen for their previous visit. Sage had considered a taxi to get them through all the traffic and decided against it. Morgan had needed to conserve her strength, they didn't.

"How long ago were you here?" Elem asked, running the dark-blue debit card through the reader to pay their entrance fee.

"It has been less than a year, yet it feels like a lifetime ago," Sage answered, taking his hand as they converged with the crowd. "Let's start with Egypt! I hope the King Tut exhibit is still here."

A portion of the pyramid which had been the burial site of King

Tutankhamun had been recreated to depict the sixteen steps which lead down to the entrance corridor of the tomb. From there a short passageway lead to the antechamber, then to the burial chamber, and lastly to the treasury, with an additional exit that wasn't in the real tomb. Colorful hieroglyphics duplicated from the originals from thousands of years ago were painted on the interior walls. They wandered along the designated path for tourists and admired the treasures. Even though the objects in view were beautiful to see, placards reminded the tourists these treasures were not real.

"It says in the brochure that everything inside here is a fake. Even so, it's roped off and guarded to prevent theft. It's meant more to display what was seen when first discovered," Elem read from the glossy hand out once they emerged from the tomb. "And of course, copies are available in the gift shop."

"The real stuff is outside of the chamber in glass cases and heavily guarded. Last time I was here we could barely get close enough to see," Sage explained.

"I'm surprised Morgan didn't make a way for you to get closer," Elem whispered to her.

"Oh, she did," Sage laughed, edging closer to the case that held the golden ankh.

"Ah, now I finally get to see what all the fuss was about back in the sixties," Elem commented. "As hippies, the ankh was a popular symbol for jewelry when we found out it was the Egyptian word for *life*. It held a spiritual meaning for us."

Sage stared at him in bewilderment.

"Sweetheart," he whispered, "Don't forget I'm still in my seventies even though I now have the body of a thirty-year-old and the memories of eight-hundred years." He paused. "I'll have you know this all feels surreal."

"It was a bit disconcerting to see the Civil War display yesterday having memories of living during that time," Elem said, running the debit card yet again to get them into the Prehistoric building later that week.

"No wonder you were so quiet over dinner. I know it's been a long week, and I'm glad we saved this building for last," Sage said. "It's one of my favorites, especially the swamp."

Once again, the Jurassic period displays and dinosaur re-creations were crowded with the curious. Several groups of children, led by a museum guide and flanked by teachers and parents, made their way along the many corridors.

The tunnel that had been turned into an Amazon-like forest was once again oddly empty. Sage and Elem leaned on the railing that separated them from the fake primordial swamp, breathing in the humidity and mossy scent. Recorded animal calls still sounded gently in the background, and the fog machine pumped out just enough mist over the shallow water to keep it mysterious. They lingered until another group of pre-teen children were ushered in, and slowly meandered toward the exit until they heard a panicked voice.

"Michael?" a woman's voice yelled.

Their exceptional hearing tuned into the conversation.

"Martha, have you seen Michael?"

"No, I thought he was with you."

"What's the problem?" the concerned voice of the museum guide asked.

"My son Michael is missing!" the panic was rising.

"Which one is he?"

"He's got dark hair, brown eyes, and is autistic!"

"Autistic? I didn't realize we had a child with special needs in the group. About ten minutes ago one of the boys had asked me where the bathroom was. I thought he had rejoined the group before we moved on. Let me call security." The guide ushered the group back out of the tunnel so her radio would work. Sage and Elem followed them out and continued to listen.

Michael's mother grew more and more concerned. "He's high functioning but too trusting and doesn't understand the danger of going off by himself," she wailed.

Several security personnel approached the group and got a description of the lost boy. The public announcement system announced the situation and asked for everyone to be on the watch for the little boy.

"Sage," Elem took her hand.

"Yes, I know," and they moved slightly away from the agitated group in the pretext of looking at one of the dinosaur models. Each of them closed their eyes and stretched out their enhanced senses to search.

"I feel several confused and crying children; two of them are boys," Elem was the first to say. "Come on." He grabbed Sage's hand, and they moved quickly away and toward another exhibit, following the muffled crying only they could hear.

As the anguish felt in his head grew stronger, Elem stopped. Ahead of them was the boy.

"There you are, Tommy! You scared me not keeping up!" Tommy's mother scolded him.

"I'm sorry, Mommy; I wanted to see the Raptors again."

Sage turned her attention the way they had come and dug deep inside, tapping into Morgan's powers. She turned slightly and said, "that way; they're heading toward the doors," she pointed toward the exit sign.

"They?" Elem questioned.

"Michael isn't alone; he's with an older man."

"Let's go!" Elem took off at a quick walk, not wanting to alarm anyone.

They approached the crowd at the massive glass doors and

zeroed in on a man holding the boy's hand tightly as the youngster tugged and whimpered.

"You will stop!" Elem growled quietly and raised his hand. The man stopped in his tracks, unable to move. Others continued to rush by, unaware of the drama playing out.

Sage searched the man's mind aggressively and he flinched in pain.

"He's a convicted pedophile! Elem, we have to do something quickly without drawing attention to ourselves," Sage said, sending out a summoning spell to the distraught mother.

Elem casually walked up to the man and said, "Oh, thank you! I see you found Michael. His mom will be really grateful." He put his hand on the pedophile's shoulder and the man let go of the scared boy's hand. Alarm, and then panic, rose in his bleary old eyes.

"Michael!" the mother called out, running up to her son and ignoring Sage and Elem. She clutched the boy in her arms and wept with relief. "Oh, I'm so glad you're okay. I was worried and scared." She hugged him again.

"I'm sorry, Momma, I had to pee, and then the nice man said he would take me back to you, so I followed him, but he got mad when I told him he was going the wrong way."

Elem kept his hand on the man's shoulder until mother and son moved away, and then scowled, sending enough of a pulse out through his hand to cause a heart attack. The sorcerer and sorceress disappeared into the throng of people and out the doors moments before the guy clutched his chest and slumped to the floor, a mere six feet from the exit.

Outside on the wide entranceway, Elem stopped and said, "I'm angry and hungry!" They walked away solemnly looking for the nearest deli.

"It was the right thing to do, Elem," Sage said, biting into the Reuben sandwich, relishing the abundance of thinly sliced corned beef and the tang of sauerkraut.

"I know it was, dear. Doesn't make it feel any better though," Elem agreed, picking up his fried egg, cheese, and coleslaw sandwich on thick slices of sourdough bread.

"I shudder at the thought of what might have happened to that boy."

"After he had been used and abused, chances are he would have been killed and left in a dumpster somewhere."

A tear trickled down Sage's cheek. "I think it's time for us to go home."

"I've never thought to ask before, Elem, but did you have children in your previous life?" Sage asked.

"No, and I never married either. I think I was waiting for you," he smiled and kissed her hand. "Why? Are you thinking we should have children?"

"No, I was just curious." Sage was silent for a few minutes. "Now that I am like I am, I could never bring a child into the world."

"Why not?"

"Oh, Elem, how would it feel to raise a child, and love him, only to watch him grow old and die while we stayed young? The emotional pain would be too hard to bear," She frowned. "It's going to be hard enough watching that happen to Jon and Lyle over the next forty years or so."

CHAPTER THIRTY EIGHT

———————— ✦ ————————

"**H**ave you seen Jon and Lyle?" Sage asked.

"I think they went out to select some drapery fabric for our new bedroom," Elem answered, looking up from the newspaper he was reading. They had been home a week since their trip to the world renown museum; the incident with the pedophile was all but forgotten.

"I thought they would be back by now. They've been gone for hours."

"Yes, but you know how they get when they're shopping...." Elem was interrupted by the doorbell.

"Excuse me," Henry said, approaching them in the library. "There's a policeman here to see you. Shall I show him in?"

"We'll see him in the greeting room," Sage looked at Elem, concerned.

"I'm sorry to intrude on your afternoon," Detective Wilkes said. "Do you know a Lyle Jones?"

"Yes, he's a close friend and lives here. Why? What's happened?" Elem spoke for the two of them.

"And a Jon Tippan?"

"Yes, yes! What's going on?" Sage pushed.

"They were attacked roughly three hours ago. Mr. Tippan suffered several cracked ribs and a concussion, and Mr. Jones is in ICU," the detective informed them. "Your name and address was listed as next of kin."

Sage and Elem stepped off the hospital elevator on the fourth floor of the hospital on the outskirts of the Upper Westside and began searching for room 452, where Jon was being kept.

Quietly entering the room, Sage approached the bed. "Jon?"

His eyes fluttered open and he smiled weakly. "Sage." Her name came out garbled through his battered and swollen mouth.

"Can you tell us what happened? The detective that came to the house was very vague," Elem said. His eyes took in the monitors hooked up to his friend and his nose wrinkled at the antiseptic smells that clung to everything. The condition of Jon's face angered and saddened him.

"We had just finished ordering the new fabric and walked around the corner looking for a cab, when four guys jumped us." Jon stopped as a wave of pain hit him. "It all happened so fast. Lyle went down, and they started kicking him. Then one of them punched me, and I saw stars. I've been in enough fights when I was a teen that instinct took over, and I fought back. Then one of them swung a baseball bat at me. I ducked when I saw it coming and he hit one of his buddies instead. I tried to help Lyle, but the one guy seemed furious I was fighting back and kept punching me in the face until I went down too. Then the three kept kicking and kicking us." He paused for a deep breath and groaned, tears dripped down the side of his bruised and beaten face.

"Okay, Jon, don't talk anymore," Elem looked at Sage and saw tears streaming down her face too. He moved and closed the door. "We'll take care of you. Sage," he looked deep into her eyes, "focus."

They set their hands on Jon's torso and emanated a blue pulsing light for several minutes. Jon groaned as the broken bones began to knit. Elem moved his hands to the cuts and bruises on Jon's face and Sage stopped him.

"There would be too many questions asked if the visible injuries are gone so quickly. Let's wait until we get him home for that," Sage said. "Jon, how are you feeling now?"

"Exhausted, but better," he pivoted his eyes and said, "Sage, they won't let me see Lyle. I'm so worried, he wasn't moving when the police showed up, and the three ran."

"Three? I thought you said there were four," Elem questioned.

"The fourth one was still out cold from being hit with the baseball bat. I overheard a nurse say he's on another floor with a concussion under police guard."

"You rest, we're going to see Lyle," Sage stated. "We'll be back soon."

"We're here to see Lyle Jones," Elem told the floor nurse outside of the Intensive Care Unit on the eighth floor.

"Sorry. He's listed as no visitors," she said and went back to her computer.

"We're his family," Sage pushed a spell with her mind, much like she had seen Morgan do. "You will let us see him."

"Yes, of course. He's in unit three. He's pretty banged up. Please don't stay too long," she looked down again.

They quietly pushed open the door to Lyle's room to find him hooked up to several monitors, an oxygen feed, and an IV. Sage inhaled sharply over the damage to his handsome face.

They stood on either side of him, like they had done to Jon, and light pulsed gently from their palms, seeking out the internal injuries. Lyle moaned.

"Oh my dear friend, what did they do to you?" Elem's lower lip quivered then stopped and Sage saw anger rising in his deep blue eyes. "Stay here with him and do what you can. I'll be back in a few minutes." He left before she could protest.

Sage put her finger on Lyle's forehead and said, "Sleep." Then she continued to send discreet healing light to his battered internal organs and cracked ribs.

Elem stepped into the elevator and closed the doors. He let his mind search for the random thoughts of a bored cop, and got out on the third floor. Down the hall, a uniformed policeman sat on a chair, playing games on his smart phone. Elem pointed a finger and convinced the man he had to use the bathroom urgently. When the officer disappeared behind the restroom door, Elem slipped into the room.

"Who are you?" the young Hispanic man asked, wincing when his facial muscles connected to the huge bruise on the side of his face.

"I'm your worst nightmare," Elem sneered. "You hurt my friends, and now I'm going to hurt yours. I want the names of the other three that were with you for the attack." His eyes bore into the man on the bed.

"Bobby Kirkland, Joe Panicara and Tommy Rodrigues," he had no choice but to tell Elem everything.

"Why did you attack those two men?"

"We were bored," he said in a monotone.

Elem seethed with anger at that answer.

"You have a headache don't you; a really bad headache; a headache so bad it feels like your brain is going to explode." A very angry Elem slipped out of the room moments before the monitors went off, alerting the nursing station that a patient had flat lined. Cause of death would be listed as a massive brain hemorrhage due to the blunt force trauma.

Sage still held Lyle's hand when Elem reentered the Intensive Care Unit.

"How's he doing?"

"Better. The internal bleeding has stopped, and the cracked ribs are healing. Again, I don't think we should do too much until we can get him home, although I did manage to reduce some of the facial swelling. The doctors are going to find he's making a remarkable recovery," Sage smiled. "He's a handsome man, and the damage to his face makes me so sad."

"It makes me angry," Elem countered.

"I noticed. Where were you?"

"One down, three to go." Elem stared out the window of the door. "Let's go see Jon and give him a progress report. Then we need to eat. Expending all this energy is making me hungry again." Sage only nodded, noticing her hands were quaking. She would find out later what he had been up to.

"Hi, how are you feeling Jon?" the doctor asked, reading the chart and barely glancing at his patient.

"I'm a bit sore, but much better. When can I go home?"

"That will depend on the care you get at home," the doctor said.

"He has us, doctor, and if he needs anything, or anyone, additional, we'll take care of it," Elem said matter-of-factly as they entered the room.

"I'd like to run another set of x-rays. The first set indicated broken ribs, and I find no evidence of that now. Once I see those, he can be discharged, most likely in the morning."

With the door closing behind the doctor, Sage took Jon's hand. "Lyle is going to be fine. I think we might even take him home soon too."

———————•✦•———————

Elem and Sage stopped at the nearest deli, ordering sandwiches with sides of coleslaw and potato salad. Sage understood now why Morgan always seemed to have a big appetite: drawing on the powers from within burned a great deal of calories.

"Where did you go when I stayed with Lyle?" Sage asked.

"I had a visit with one of the attackers and got the names of the other three," he replied taking a big bite of his pastrami and salami sandwich.

Sage raised her eyebrows. "And what are you going to do with that information?"

"I'm not sure yet," he confessed. "I want Jon and Lyle home first...maybe."

"Maybe?"

"Laid up in a hospital bed is a perfect alibi."

CHAPTER THIRTY NINE

———•——✷——•———

E lem had the cab drop him in front of the now closed fabric shop where Jon and Lyle had been attacked and started walking in a tight grid around that location. He pressed further and further out, the neighborhoods becoming more and more dismal the wider his search became, until he spotted a cluster of three young men sitting on the broken, steep steps of a crumbling apartment building, drinking beer and whiskey from bottles wrapped in brown paper bags. He stretched his senses to hear their comments.

"Poor Eddie; I can't believe he's dead."

"He wouldn't be if you hadn't hit him with the bat," someone replied.

"Hey, that one guy ducked. It's his fault Eddie is dead! I'm going to find him and kill him…slow…real slow."

Elem walked up to the small group and stood twenty feet away, watching.

"Who are you, and what are you looking at, gringo?" Tommy said with a drunken sneer.

"I do believe I've found who I'm looking for: Bobby, Joe, and Tommy, right?" Elem barely controlled his rage at finding those responsible for the injuries inflicted on his friends.

"What's it to ya?" another one, Joe, stood ready for a fight. "Maybe *you* want some of our steel-toed boots!" They all laughed.

"You hurt my friends because you were bored. *Bored!*" Elem repeated, raising his voice. "I can't let you get away with that."

"So what are you going to do, eh? Turn us over to the cops?" they laughed again.

"No, they will likely keep you overnight and let you go after charges are filed. Assault-and-battery charges are common for thugs like you, aren't they? Then, you will be back on the streets as if nothing happened," Elem smiled and shook his head sadly. When he looked up, all three had stood and were descending the stoop steps coming at him. "I didn't say you could move!" and Elem held up one hand, sending them back a few feet.

"What the f…." Tommy managed to squeak out. "Who *are* you?"

"*What* are you?" Joe said, starting to shake yet he was unable to move even his feet.

"I'll tell you the same thing I told Eddie. I'm your worst nightmare," Elem's voice had taken on a deadly, menacing tone. "Mother told me I should fight evil with kindness, but she didn't say kindness to whom. Maybe this time the kindness is to those you won't be able to hurt anymore." He pointed at Tommy. "You were going to bash in Jon's head and likely kill him, but you missed. I don't miss." He sent out a single ball of lightning, catching Tommy square in the chest, who then collapsed. Two more balls of lightning found their targets. All three lay dead on the steps, their hearts had simply stopped. Elem turned away, his fury abated. The bodies would be found quick enough.

———◦✺◦———

The sun was starting to set when Elem opened the front door. Sage flew into his arms and hugged him tightly.

"Even though you said not to worry, I still did!" Sage said. "Where did you go?"

Elem followed her into the library where he fixed himself a

strong drink and sat in front of the heatless fire Sage had created. It was good for ambiance without raising the temperature of the room already warmed by the summer afternoon sun.

"I took care of a problem," he said, downing his drink and fixing another.

"Should I ask Alyce to fix you something to eat?"

"Please, I'm famished," he answered, closing his eyes and resting his head on the back of the padded chair.

When she returned, carrying a platter full of fried chicken, she said, "Talk to me."

He looked at the woman he loved; a woman who was more than a wife to him, she was his other half, his soul mate, and he hoped she understood.

"I killed them. All of them."

"And?" Sage said matter-of-factly. "Am I supposed to be upset? I'm not, Elem. They hurt, and almost killed, our best friends! Those four thugs are, or were, the darker side of society, and we're better off without them."

Elem set down the chicken leg he was about to bite into, and pulled Sage into his arms, kissing her soundly.

"So how did they die?"

"I took care of Eddie in the hospital. His mild concussion apparently was misdiagnosed, and he suffered a major, and fatal, hemorrhage in his brain."

Sage nodded.

"Those other three had heart failure, and while it will initially seem odd for men so young, the authorities will look for traces of an unknown substance in the booze they were drinking. They won't find anything though."

She nodded again.

"I know I should feel bad, but I don't. I overheard them talking, and they blamed Jon for Eddie's death and were going to hunt him down and kill him for ducking." Elem put down the bone from the fourth piece of chicken and dug into the macaroni on his plate; the carbohydrates quickly absorbed by his metabolism.

"Elem, there are bad people out there that while they may not deserve to die, they also don't deserve to live. You did what you needed to do to protect not only Jon and Lyle, but others who might have fallen prey to those guys." Sage poured a glass of wine for herself. "Oh, and the hospital called: we can pick Jon up tomorrow morning...after we settle the bill of course," she smiled. "The doctor also called and was beside himself at the progress Lyle has made. He thinks we can bring Lyle home the day after tomorrow."

"It makes me angry that this even happened, Sage," Elem pushed his food aside.

"Me too, dear, and I've been thinking about how we can avoid this from happening again," she answered. "I'd like to buy something like a limo and hire a driver. With four of us it would be a practical expense."

"I think that's an excellent idea."

"I was also talking to Henry about housekeeping. It was something I never thought much about when Morgan was...still alive," Sage sighed deeply. "With there being only her for so long, Henry said they had a cleaning service in once a week. With four of us now, we should have a live-in."

"That's another good idea."

"I'm glad you think so, because I've already contacted an employment agency to find us a husband and wife team," Sage smiled at Elem's shock. "Hey, I had to do *some*thing while you were out... taking care of business."

He laughed. "When do we start the interviews?"

"It may take a while to find the right pair, and if it takes too long, we can adjust and get two individuals."

CHAPTER FORTY

———————— ❈ ————————

"Jon, you saw for yourself that Lyle is doing fine. Besides, he'll be home tomorrow, and you can talk with him then," Sage reminded him. "How are your ribs feeling?"

"What you and Elem did was remarkable, Sage, truly remarkable," Jon said. "The pain was everywhere in my body, and now, it's only in my face."

"Let's get you upstairs to bed and I'll fix your face," she smiled lovingly at him. "You still need to rest, and I'm finding it's easier to... repair damage when you're asleep and not resisting or trying to help."

Jon reluctantly went up the stairs and to his room, with Sage following.

"But I'm hungry. That hospital food is awful!" he complained.

"You can eat later, and I promise to wake you for dinner. Your body needs to work at healing and not at digesting—now, bed!" she pointed at the oversized bed that reigned in the spacious room. After he lay down, she touched his forehead, and he fell into a deep sleep. Sage spent a full half hour healing the fractured cheek bones and the bruises that dominated the left side of Jon's face, and then she went in search for food herself.

———————— ❈ ————————

Sage found Elem and Will in the kitchen discussing cabinets and countertops with an overwrought Alyce, who was flustered at having so many in her domain.

"You really should decide what you want, Alyce," Will was coaxing the reluctant cook into choosing marble, slate, or hardwood countertops.

"What's the problem?" Sage asked, opening the refrigerator and bringing out a bowl full of leftover macaroni. She put it in the microwave to reheat and turned to the group.

"I don't want to make a decision without Mr. Jon!" Alyce protested.

"Then don't," Sage turned to Will and said, "can't you take all the measurements and work on the layout without certain specifics? Jon will be up and around tomorrow, Alyce, and we can wait until then."

"Yes, ma'am, boss-lady," Will said with a smile. He knew who was writing the checks. "I'll bring samples over tomorrow for everyone to look at." As he let himself out the side door, someone rang the front doorbell.

"Excuse me, Miss Sage, that Detective Wilkes is here again. He's waiting in the greeting room."

"What can we do for you, Detective Wilkes? Do you have any leads on the attackers?" Elem asked straight faced when they walked into the frequently used room.

"Yes, and no," the detective paced. "The one we had in custody died yesterday afternoon from his head injury, and, unfortunately, before I could question him regarding the others."

"That's a shame. I would like to have seen him stand trial for what he did," Elem said.

"So there are no leads to the others?" Sage said with a frown.

"That's where the yes and no come in," he answered with his

own frown. "With the ID of the now deceased perp, we were able to track down his known associates."

"That's good news, right?" Elem said.

"It is, but the bad news is those three are dead."

"What?" Elem and Sage said together.

"And that's why I'm here. With the two victims in the hospital at the time, they're in the clear; however, I do need to ask where you two were yesterday late afternoon."

"We've both been here since we arrived home from the hospital. Why? Are we suspects?" Elem asked with a chuckle.

"Other than the victims, you two are the only ones with a possible grudge."

"Unless, this isn't the first time they've beat up someone," Sage said frowning, and effectively re-directing the detective's focus.

"It's possible there have been other instances," the detective agreed just before his phone chirped with an incoming text message. He read it quickly and put the phone back in his pocket. "That was the coroner's office. The autopsies have been completed. Cause of death for all three was heart failure, which of course is strange for such young men. The other oddity is there are no—and I mean zero—indications of any physical trauma, other than they are dead; their hearts just stopped. Toxicology reports are being run now." He ran his fingers through his thinning dark hair. "Likely there will be some kind of drugs involved that caused their deaths. My apologies for disturbing you." He turned to leave. "I sincerely hope your friends recover quickly and don't suffer any lingering injuries."

"Don't worry, sweetheart, even if anyone saw me, which no one did, it would be easy to erase their memory like I did with the cab driver," Elem comforted Sage.

"How do you know no one saw you?"

"I used a concealment spell and lowered it only to those three." He smiled. "I'm finding it interesting how quickly I'm remembering all that Haedre taught us, even though that was eight hundred years ago. Evon was a very good student."

"I'm curious, Elem, do you remember everything from your previous...lives?"

"No, not everything, the important things, yes, and those mostly involve the time around *you*. The mundane is quite blurry though." He took her hands. "I remember how Edward felt the tickling of Evon's memory when he saw the star stone, and how he fell in love with you. He was so distraught when he found out you had been kidnapped. He nearly beat the servant that had arranged it. Instead, his goodness prevailed, and he banished the servant from the household instead.

"And I remember that Ethan fell in love with you at first sight, and I certainly don't blame him, I did too. I think Ethan's talent for dancing was a hold-over for me, and a good thing too since it brought you back into my arms. Every time they—and I—saw the star stone, more and more came back. *You and I* were meant to be."

"What became of Beatrice?" Sage asked.

"The little girl? Mary became very attached to her, having lost her entire family in the fire. She taught Bea how to cook and bake, and the girl had quite a knack for it. In turn, Bea brought Mary out of her shell. That stepmother left town shortly after we rescued the girl, and the father never did come back as far as I know. I really don't remember much more about Edward; he died a few years later," Elem told her.

"How?"

"He gave up and stopped living."

CHAPTER FORTY ONE

"**L**yle! Until we can complete your healing you are going to *have* to rest!" Sage admonished him when he wanted to help Jon with the new kitchen decisions.

"I feel so much better though," he protested. Elem and Sage brought Lyle home from the hospital early afternoon, after the doctor had given them explicit instructions on his care. In spite of the fact that Lyle had made amazing progress, the doctor had wanted to keep him a few more days because of his still battered face.

"You are going upstairs right now, and will sleep for two or three hours while I restore your handsome face," she said, tenderly touching his cheek. "All these bruises are scaring Jon *and* Alyce, and Alyce has promised to fix your favorite meal for dinner tonight."

"Really? What?"

"She won't tell me."

"It's only been a week since the guys were attacked," Elem commented, "Do you think they are healed enough for this?" They were watching the two men engage in a rather energetic game of tennis on the small court opposite the garden dome.

"As long as they don't put a ball through the glass," Sage answered.

"I thought you put a force field around it," he whispered back.

"I did, but don't tell them that. Thinking they might break something has them going a bit slower," she laughed. "Hard to believe Lyle was in critical care last week, isn't it?"

"Come on, let's see how Will is doing in the kitchen."

As they passed by the foyer, the doorbell rang. Out of habit, Sage opened the massive wooden door.

"Yes?" she said to the somewhat familiar stranger and wondered how he got through the front gate.

"Hi, I'm Doctor Davis. Forgive me for showing up like this, but I was in the neighborhood, and I thought I would check up on Lyle," he said then looked down. "No, that's a lie. I wasn't in the neighborhood. I took a cab all the way across town just to see him," he confessed. "May I come in?"

"Did Lyle miss an appointment?" Elem asked.

"No, he didn't. When my office called to set one, he said he was doing fine and hung up on her," Doctor Davis explained. "I'm concerned about him."

"That's not like Lyle to be rude. Elem, would you show the doctor to the library, and I'll get Lyle," Sage smiled to cover her unease.

Sage let herself out through the garden room and walking over to the tennis court stopped the ball in mid-flight.

"Lyle dear, your doctor is here to see you," she said, letting the ball drop harmlessly to the ground.

"Hey, I'm fine, nary even a bruise," he protested.

"He will become a problem if he doesn't get to see you," she frowned. "And no lingering bruises could be an even bigger problem. Sit over here, and let me add a few. Don't worry, once he's gone, I'll take them away again." With careful thought, she produced a fading blue bruise on his chin, two yellowed bruises on his cheek and a healing split lip. "You too, Jon. Even if he isn't your doctor, he might have seen how badly *you* were beaten while you were unconscious." She put a long fading yellow bruise across his temple and down the side of his handsome face.

—◆—❋—◆—

"While I appreciate your concern, Doctor Davis, it wasn't necessary to come all this way. I'm really doing fine," Lyle apologized.

"I can see that." He shined his penlight into Lyle's blue eyes. "No sign of the concussion, and the bruises are all but gone. You have a remarkable rate of healing." Doctor Davis turned to Sage, "May I ask what you've been doing for him?"

"Magic!" She smiled, then laughed when everyone looked startled. "The magic of love, plus organic cucumber masks for the swelling, green tea to soothe his trauma, and vitamin E oil on the cuts to speed healing and prevent scarring."

"Well, whatever it is, it's been miraculous. If I hadn't seen him in the ICU eight days ago on death's doorstep, I would not believe this is the same man."

"He's also got an incredible constitution, doctor, and he's had only natural, organic food since he's been home. I'm a firm believer in giving the body the tools it needs to heal itself," Sage said.

—◆—❋—◆—

"I've been thinking," Elem leaned back in the overstuffed chair, his evening meal now an empty plate. "Although I may have ended five lives by eliminating those attackers and the pedophile, we saved three and quite likely others. Think of all the good we can do, all the lives we could save!"

"Yes," Sage said thoughtfully, "but we shouldn't, Elem. There are people, men, women, even children, who are meant to die as a matter of their own karmic growth. That's one of the things I learned during the travels Morgan sent me on. I could *not* interfere with the past for fear of upsetting the future. And right now, *we* are the future's past."

"Then what do you suggest we do?"

Sage smiled and said, "Go with the flow and follow where it leads us."

The two ethereal beings sat on a wild-flower-filled, grassy hill that didn't exist.

"So what did you think of your life, your very *long* life, as a corporeal being, Morgan?"

"It was both good and bad, Mother. For centuries I let the power control me, instead of the other way around, and I hurt so many people for the fun of it. Only, it wasn't really fun at all and served to make me feel even worse, until..."

"Until?" Haedre asked.

"Until I met the soul of a truly nice person: the Sage spirit. After that, I tried to make amends, although I couldn't change what had already been done, and that ate away at me. I changed my ways, but in some ways, it was too late. I wandered the land trying to do good things. However, there was still so much evil it was hard not to get caught up in it sometimes. I worry about what will happen to me if I reincarnate."

"You will always have a choice in that, child. Take your time to understand what you have learned, then decide if you want to go back. That's what I did."

"Did you really take seven hundred years to contemplate your life, before coming back as Helen?"

"Yes, and it was quite enlightening, and for all the perceived bad things I did as a sorceress, it was a wonderful experience to incarnate as someone as nice and kind as Helen. Although I had no memories of my past while I was her, I know now I chose her so I could watch *your* progress."

"And Evon, does he now remember all of the incarnations he's been through? That must be very confusing to him." The spirit Morgan picked a bright yellow wild flower for her dark hair, and immediately grew another to take its place.

"Ah, my sweet Evon, now there is a good soul. He remembers only his last three lives, those that led him to Sage—his reward for his goodness. The ones before that were very short lives; he was too good, too kind to last in such violent times."

"Mother, what are those golden eggs for—the ones the serpents left behind?"

"Those are the children Sage and Elem are afraid to have. They need not worry, though; the children will continue *their* legacy and will bring them much joy. In time they will realize this."

"One more question, Mother. How long will they stay in these corporeal bodies they have?"

"As long as they want."

ABOUT THE AUTHOR

---⊷⊛⊶---

Deborah Moore is single and lives a quiet life in the Upper Peninsula of Michigan. She was in Detroit, moved to a small town to raise her two sons, and then moved to an even smaller town to pursue her dreams of being self-sufficient and to explore her love of writing. Now on her tenth published book in three years, Deborah has found that dreams do come true and she is enjoying life more than ever.

PERMUTED PRESS
needs **you** to help

SPREAD (THE) INFECTION

FOLLOW US!

f | Facebook.com/PermutedPress
🐦 | Twitter.com/PermutedPress

REVIEW US!

Wherever you buy our book, they can be reviewed! We want to know what you like!

GET INFECTED!

Sign up for our mailing list at
PermutedPress.com

PERMUTED
PRESS

KING ARTHUR AND THE KNIGHTS OF THE ROUND TABLE HAVE BEEN REBORN TO SAVE THE WORLD FROM THE CLUTCHES OF MORGANA WHILE SHE PROPELS OUR MODERN WORLD INTO THE MIDDLE AGES.

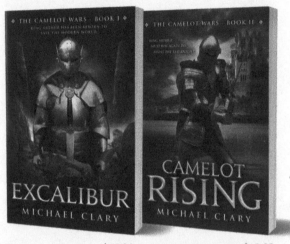

EAN 9781618685018 $15.99   EAN 9781682611562 $15.99

Morgana's first attack came in a red fog that wiped out all modern technology. The entire planet was pushed back into the middle ages. The world descended into chaos.

But hope is not yet lost— King Arthur, Merlin, and the Knights of the Round Table have been reborn.

THE ULTIMATE PREPPER'S ADVENTURE.
THE JOURNEY BEGINS HERE!

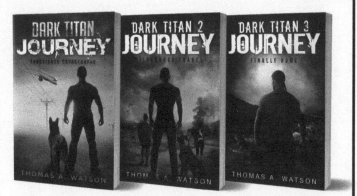

EAN 9781682611654 $9.99   EAN 9781618687371 $9.99   EAN 9781618687395 $9.99

The long-predicted Coronal Mass Ejection has finally hit the Earth, virtually destroying civilization. Nathan Owens has been prepping for a disaster like this for years, but now he's a thousand miles away from his family and his refuge. He'll have to employ all his hard-won survivalist skills to save his current community, before he begins his long journey through doomsday to get back home.

PERMUTED
PRESS

THE MORNINGSTAR STRAIN HAS BEEN LET LOOSE——IS THERE ANY WAY TO STOP IT?

An industrial accident unleashes some of the Morningstar Strain. The

EAN 9781618686497 $16.00

doctor who discovered the strain and her assistant will have to fight their way through Sprinters and Shamblers to save themselves, the vaccine, and the base. Then they discover that it wasn't an accident at all—somebody inside the facility did it on purpose. The war with the RSA and the infected is far from over.

This is the fourth book in Z.A. Recht's The Morningstar Strain series, written by Brad Munson.

GATHERED TOGETHER AT LAST, THREE TALES OF FANTASY CENTERING AROUND THE MYSTERIOUS CITY OF SHADOWS...ALSO KNOWN AS CHICAGO.

EAN 9781682612286 $9.99   **EAN** 9781618684639 $5.99   **EAN** 9781618684899 $5.99

From *The New York Times* and *USA Today* bestselling author Richard A. Knaak comes three tales from Chicago, the City of Shadows. Enter the world of the Grey–the creatures that live at the edge of our imagination and seek to be real. Follow the quest of a wizard seeking escape from the centuries-long haunting of a gargoyle. Behold the coming of the end of the world as the Dutchman arrives.

Enter the City of Shadows.

PERMUTED
PRESS

WE CAN'T GUARANTEE THIS GUIDE WILL SAVE YOUR LIFE. BUT WE CAN GUARANTEE IT WILL KEEP YOU SMILING WHILE THE LIVING DEAD ARE CHOWING DOWN ON YOU.

EAN 9781618686695 $9.99

This is the only tool you need to survive the zombie apocalypse.

OK, that's not really true. But when the SHTF, you're going to want a survival guide that's not just geared toward day-to-day survival. You'll need one that addresses the essential skills for true nourishment of the human spirit. Living through the end of the world isn't worth a damn unless you can enjoy yourself in any way you want. (Except, of course, for anything having to do with abuse. We could never condone such things. At least the publisher's lawyers say we can't.)

PERMUTED
PRESS